DESCENT

OF THE

VILE

CHERYL PEÑA

This is a work of fiction. Names, characters, places, and incidents are products of the author's imagination or are used fictitiously and are not to be construed as real. Any resemblance to actual events, locations, organizations, or persons, living or dead, is entirely coincidental.

World Castle Publishing, LLC
Pensacola, Florida
Copyright © Cheryl Peña 2022
Hardback ISBN: 9798366632089
Paperback ISBN: 9781958336984
eBook ISBN: 9781958336991
First Edition World Castle Publishing, LLC, December 20, 2022
http://www.worldcastlepublishing.com

Licensing Notes

Cover: Cheryl Peña
Editor: Karen Fuller

For my father, Alfredo Peña.
Thank you for everything you've done for me and for everything
you still do.

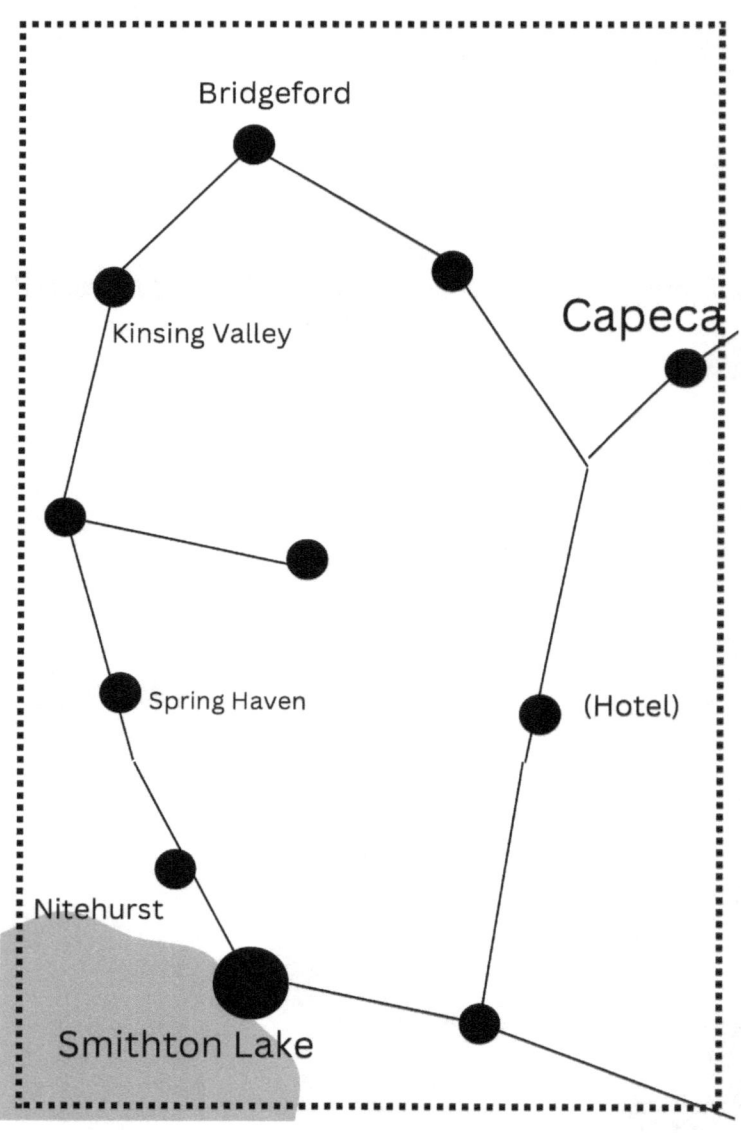

Bridgeford

Capeca

Kinsing Valley

Spring Haven

(Hotel)

Nitehurst

Smithton Lake

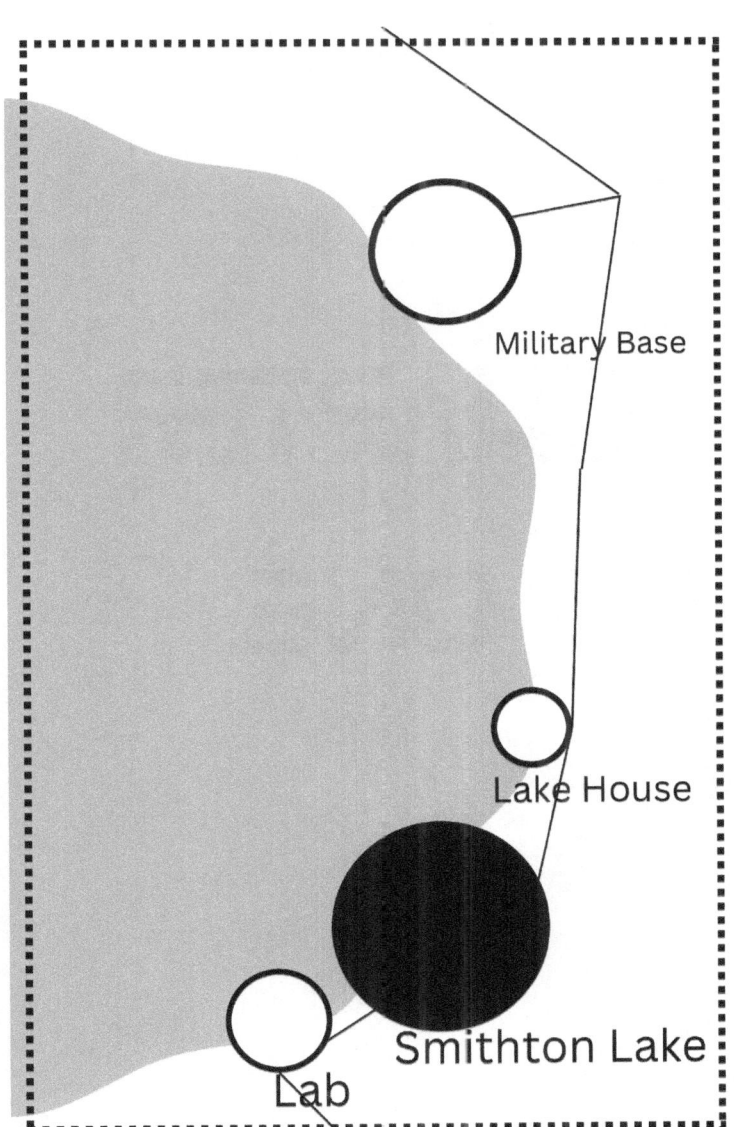

Military Base

Lake House

Smithton Lake

Lab

CHAPTER ONE

Jackson Riley was already sweating and irritable as he pulled the large metal case out of his car and set it on the ground beside him. Next, he removed the luggage rack he used to transport it and secured the case to the apparatus with the bungee cords that he perpetually kept wrapped around it. The case held his monorail 4x5 view camera that he used in his work as a freelance photographer whenever he needed exceptionally high-definition images. Although it was unwieldy, it was his favorite camera because it took such beautiful photographs. He'd even brought the adapter for his digital SLR so that he didn't need to carry film holders, extra sheet film, a dark bag, and other such equipment. But the amount of effort required to take the photographs was the same, and he felt it was worth any trouble to obtain those types of pictures.

Lastly, he removed his steel tripod from the trunk of the car and strapped it to the top of the camera case. He'd completed this routine so many times that he could balance it properly on the first try, and the case didn't roll. Once he had his equipment ready, he closed the vehicle doors and secured the locks. Turning in the direction of the large building complex past the sprawling parking lot, he realized he'd taken too long to catch the shuttle as he saw it driving away. Sighing, he set out for the far side of the campus, where several short red-brick buildings waited in the sun, knowing he had a fairly long trek ahead of him. The cart's wheels made scraping noises on the concrete behind him, rolling through the gravel and loose dirt as he walked.

The further he went, the more he wished he had caught the shuttle. Even with the cart, the protective case was heavy, and his hands were sweating within minutes. The heat radiated off the concrete and burned into his feet and legs, and the glare from the sun caused him to squint, reminding him he'd forgotten sunglasses, as usual. Briefly, he considered removing his black blazer but then changed his mind, wanting to keep a professional appearance. However, he started to breathe heavily in the humidity, and he wondered if he would get a sunburn on the back of his neck. Annoyingly inconvenient also, he had to weave around because sometimes there would be a large truck or a car parked crookedly, and he couldn't fit the case between the vehicles. It was time-consuming and exhausting.

He continued walking until he reached the concourse and looked around to orient himself. His contact, Devin, was supposed to meet him there to escort him to the correct office, but he didn't see anyone. Looking around for someone who appeared to be waiting for him, he saw a man and a woman approach him from under an overhead walkway where they had been standing in the shade.

"Are you Mr. Riley?" the man said.

"Yes. Devin?" Jackson asked.

The man shook his hand. "Devin Blair. This is Keira Hastings," he introduced his colleague from the lab. Keira was stunningly beautiful, but she also seemed to be all too sure of that fact. Her haughty demeanor was evident even as she greeted him.

Jackson shook her hand also and wished he could hurry them to the air-conditioning without being rude. He knew his palm was damp, and he could feel sweat dripping down the sides of his face and down his back.

They seemed oblivious to his discomfort and gave him a lecture about the history of the lab and a rundown of what types of photographs they needed. Of course, he had already heard this before and didn't know why they were repeating themselves. But they were walking slowly as they turned to look at him and gesticulated to emphasize certain words. He nodded and tried to listen politely.

Eventually, they led him to one of the red brick buildings, about five stories tall, with modern glass windows and doors, the Geiger BioTech lab logo etched into the glass. Devin held the door for him too briefly before heading inside, leaving Jackson to try to catch it and pull the camera case through behind him simultaneously. He would have attempted a glare, but they were already ahead of him at the elevators, waiting after pressing the "up" button. Luckily, he made it to those before the doors opened, but this time, Keira held her hand on the door to allow everyone to board the car. It seemed almost an afterthought like she was holding the door for Devin, but Jackson just happened to be there.

When they arrived at the third floor, Devin and Keira took him to an office, again with heavy frosted glass doors and chrome fixtures, holding the door only long enough for Jackson to grasp it with his own hand and then releasing it as if they didn't realize the camera case was an encumbrance and he needed extra help. He clumsily pulled the case through and into the space on his own, although he had to leave it in the outer office, as there wasn't enough room where he would be working. So, he unstrapped the tripod and opened the case to remove the large camera. Carefully holding it by the rail and trying to keep it upright, he carried it and the tripod toward the double glass doors of the small lab. Devin and Keira were still talking to him, although they weren't looking at him as they walked inside. But this time, Jackson wasn't quite quick enough to make it in behind them. He barely caught the leaden glass and metal monstrosity before it could crash into the lens of the camera, trying to brace the door with his foot while also extending his fingers in a desperate attempt to keep it away from the valuable optics. Obviously, he didn't have a free hand to open the thing any further.

"Hey!" he called out, still trying to hold the door. They didn't seem to hear him. "Can I get some help, please?" he shouted louder.

Keira impatiently jerked the door from his hand and allowed him to enter with the bulky camera. She said nothing as she crossed, again, to the other side of the small room, but she gave him a scowl as he tried to set the tripod down with one hand without letting go of the rail on the camera. He wondered why they were suddenly so irritable. They hadn't been in a rush outside, but now they seemed to be making up for lost time.

"I'm sorry, but this equipment is fairly expensive and is not easy to replace," he said by way of an explanation. They didn't seem to care that he'd spoken. He sighed again.

Carefully setting the camera on the floor, he opened the heavy stainless-steel tripod and extended the legs, then picked the camera up and secured it to the top. He had a lighter aluminum tripod at home, but it wasn't sturdy enough for that particular camera, only for his press camera and field camera. Next, he removed his jacket and draped it over the back of the camera and over his head to create a dark space to see properly while he extended the bellows part way to compose the upside-down image on the ground glass.

Devin and Keira helped him to determine what he needed to do, then left him to work. Jackson continued to use the ground glass to compose his image and then to focus the camera. Then, he returned to the outer office to pick up his DSLR and the adapter out of the case, taking those in with him to his workspace. Once he had composed and focused his image, he then removed the ground glass and inserted the adapter, then secured the DSLR to the adapter. To take the series of six photos necessary to compose the image, he removed the adapter after each shot to reposition it. Then, he removed the DSLR and adapter altogether to compose another image on the ground glass. He would need to process the photos and stitch them together digitally in Photoshop later, but for that moment, he just wanted to take his shots and leave. Ideally, he would have used a digital back for the camera, but he didn't usually have the space to work with one and didn't think it was worth the expense for his particular schedule as he wasn't called to use it often enough. And he preferred film when he was shooting for pleasure.

Devin and Keira were becoming impatient again, as if they were expecting the entire set of pictures to be done in a few minutes. When Keira checked on Jackson later, he let her know it would still be quite a while for him to finish. After the day he'd had so far, he definitely didn't want to come back, so he took his time and tried not to rush. They didn't seem to understand the amount of effort involved, although he remembered trying to explain it all over the phone before his actual arrival.

The sun was setting outside the window, and he tried not to become agitated. He didn't understand what was so important about the items they gave him to know why they wanted the images in high definition, but it wasn't his job to argue. He didn't even know what the items were. The fact that Devin and Keira couldn't explain it very well made him wonder if they knew either. Some of the objects looked very old, but others looked new, and although they didn't look like anything he had seen before, they were very ordinary-looking. It all seemed very mundane. He didn't understand the urgency or why they would only allow him to shoot in that tiny lab. Fortunately, given that Devin treated the objects like precious jewels or fragile butterfly wings, Jackson was glad he had thought to bring cotton gloves, like the kind used in handling valuable artwork or archaeological artifacts, to move the objects and reposition them when needed.

Devin and Keira both seemed upset at having to stay late (as if this were something Jackson found preferable), but in the end, only Devin remained. Keira departed just before the stars started to come out as Jackson painstakingly went through the "catalogue" of objects and photographed them from the different angles that had all been described to him, finishing the last one as Devin checked his watch for the hundredth time.

Carefully, Jackson took the equipment apart and carried it out to his case for storage and transport. That time, however, Devin seemed to realize that it would be faster if he held the door for Jackson to get everything out of the lab. So, it was quicker to dismantle the assembly than to set it all up. Jackson gingerly stored the camera and other equipment in the case, locked it, and then secured it to the luggage rack he had used to carry everything to the third-floor office.

Lastly, he retrieved his tripod and waited for Devin to lock the door and escort him back down to ground level.

"Can you find your way out?" Devin asked. "The last shuttle should be leaving soon."

"Yes, thank you," Jackson replied, trying not to allow

any resentment to color his tone, although he was annoyed that Devin wouldn't escort him back. Trying to ignore the headache that threatened to explode on him shortly, he hurried across the concourse in the semi-darkness, hoping to catch the shuttle this time around. A few floodlights scattered around the complex barely illuminated the area with their sodium-yellow glow. However, even though the sun had gone down, it was only marginally cooler than in the afternoon. As he reached the edge of the complex, he saw the shuttle driving away, to his utter disappointment. Frustrated, he rushed to chase it down, determined not to miss it again, barely reaching it and knocking on the back door to get the driver to stop. The shuttle slowed and then came to a halt, and Jackson felt relieved that he wouldn't have to walk the entire way back to his car toward the back of the expansive parking lot.

The doors opened, and he checked behind him to see that he was able to bring the view camera case up onto the bottom step. Then he looked up, unable to believe what he saw. Every one of the occupants had a horrifying, ragged appearance, some of them with open wounds or blisters covering their exposed skins. A few of them were twitching in a manner that seemed almost mechanical, as if a machine were malfunctioning. Their blank stares turned toward him, and they watched him as he froze, not knowing what to do or what would happen. Somehow, he could sense that they saw him as an outsider and that he didn't belong there. Holding his breath, not daring to move, he could hear his heartbeat pounding in his ears. Then, they advanced on him. Although they didn't move quickly, he knew he was in danger. He was still standing against the door and had no space to retreat, so he yanked the emergency brake cord, backing out of the shuttle down the steps, tripping over the camera case and tumbling out onto the concrete below. Ignoring his scraped arms, he only very briefly considered grabbing the camera case but bolted away instead, knowing he didn't have time.

Running away, he saw more of the slow-moving, ragged-looking people ambling toward him from the direction he'd just come from, possibly hundreds of them. He sprinted across the parking lot, searching for his car in the nighttime gloom, and he only found it because it was situated under a floodlight. Panicking, he quickly found his keys in his pocket, but he dropped them in his haste to unlock the car. Frantically, he picked them up again and opened the door, starting the ignition as he looked for the exit. Then, he gunned the engine and raced away from the buildings.

Where had these people come from? He hadn't seen them upon his arrival and had never seen such things in his life. This can't be real, he told himself. This can't be real. But, as he drove out of the lot, he saw more of them. Most of them seemed to be moving in one direction, toward the city, so he tried to drive in the opposite one.

The building complex was built on the edge of the city of Smithton Lake, and he sped away toward the larger four-lane road that led out of the city. It was not a highway, but he suddenly had to be careful as there were other cars fleeing whatever disaster was unfolding. Most of them weren't being very cautious and were speeding away, but Jackson carefully merged with the other traffic. He drove as quickly as he could down the crowded street, seeing more of the strange people in the middle of the road and off to the sides, slowly moving toward Smithton Lake. Some of them seemed to lurch toward the cars as they passed.

The further away he got, it seemed that there were fewer of them, but he didn't know where they had come from to know where he needed to go. He just knew he had to get away from there. But as he continued to drive, he could see that although there were fewer strange people, there were still a lot of them. What if there were some in the next town, also? Still, he had no choice but to go there. It was his only route out.

He swerved away from the strangers as he encountered them on the road, but in the dark, they were somewhat hard to spot. His headlights illuminated them only moments before he would reach them, and he was upset that he had to slow down slightly. Then, he saw a person in the road up ahead trying to leap in front of the car that preceded his as the car abruptly veered around. The closer he got to the pedestrian, however, he could see that it was a terrified woman trying to commit suicide rather than let the strangers get to her. As he got closer, she tried to leap in front of his car, but he managed to swerve away, saying, "No, no, no, no," distressingly to himself as he pulled the car off the road. There were still too many of the strangers nearby, and he didn't know if he could get to her in time, but he opened his door, then hurried back toward her, seeing her lunge at the next car behind his. When he reached her, he quickly grabbed her and pulled her away as she screamed and wept.

"No, get in the car. I'll get you away," he urged her. The traffic stream continued past them, but he hoped she would come with him. He gestured toward his car, and she nodded, swiftly running toward the passenger door, which he opened from the inside as he reached the driver's side. A couple of the strangers had almost reached his car, and he had to reverse a short distance to merge into traffic once again.

Still fearful, Jackson wove around the strange people as much as he could until there were hardly any, except a few off to the sides of the road and in the neighboring fields. Thinking about stopping for the night, he had no idea where it might be safe. It was several miles to Nitehurst, and he knew there was a real possibility that he might need to go farther still.

"Do you know what happened?" Jackson asked his scared passenger.

She shook her head, still in tears.

"Where did those people come from?" he asked himself. "Who are they? What do they want?"

She sat still, not answering. Maybe she didn't know either.

He sighed. "I'm sorry. I know this isn't your fault. I'm going to go to Nitehurst. I hope we'll be safer there, at least until we can figure something out. Unless you have somewhere else to go?" He looked expectantly at her.

She shook her head again.

He turned his gaze back to the road. "What's your name?" he asked her.

Although she appeared confused, her tears were slowing. She just looked extremely traumatized and like it didn't seem to matter, at that point, what happened to her.

"My name's Jackson," he told her. "What's yours?"

She seemed to snap out of her trance. "Nadine." She sniffed and wiped a strand of shoulder-length black hair back from her dark eyes. Looking up at him, she gave him a small smile, but it was gone as soon as it had appeared. If he had blinked, he would have missed it, and he still wasn't sure, at that point, if it had been there at all.

"What do you think? I know it might not be any safer in Nitehurst." He kept looking at the road.

"I don't know."

Partially, he was afraid to ask but he finally posed the question. "What were you doing out there on the road?"

Vehemently, she shook her head. "I don't want to think about it."

"No. I mean, how did you get there? What happened to you?"

Looking suddenly like she might start crying again, she took a deep breath as the tears began anew. "They came into my house. I was almost asleep. But I heard the door, and I went to check it out. I saw one of them in the kitchen. Then suddenly, there were more of them. Lots more. I climbed out of the window and ran, but there were just too many. I didn't think I could get away. I ran through the fields and into the trees and kept going. But when I made it to the road, it was worse. I didn't know what to do."

He looked down and saw that she didn't have any shoes and her feet were bloody from cuts and scrapes. There were abrasions on her knees and hands from falling on the road and from scrambling through the mud. "Do you need a doctor?"

She shook her head.

He wasn't sure about that, but he didn't press the issue. "So, who or what are they? Have you seen them before?"

"No," she replied.

He sighed. "I want to know what this is about."

———

As he drove further and further from the metropolitan area around Smithton Lake, he hoped they would be safer. There were still some of the strangers out in the fields or in the trees when they were finally away from the farms. But the strangers were no longer in large crowds anymore, and there were smaller numbers the further they went. By the time they reached Nitehurst, he could have almost convinced himself it was just a nightmare. But Nadine was still in his car, and he couldn't explain that occurrence to himself any other way. Nitehurst was a very small town and only had a few hotels. He drove off the main road and into the town to find a more hidden inn, down narrow streets toward a small hotel that rested next to a creek which was mostly dry in the summer. Then, he drove into the tiny lot to the side of the old white stone-fronted three-story building and parked the car as close to the door as he could get.

"Do you want to wait here?" he asked.

"No." She looked alarmed.

"Okay. I'll get a couple of rooms. Follow me." They walked to the front entrance, where Jackson held the door for Nadine, then he entered the building behind her.

The tall wooden reception desk looked deserted, and he wondered what had happened, if the strangers had already been there before them. But eventually, an older grey-haired man came out of the office behind the desk and up to the first monitor. "Can I help you?" the man asked.

"Er...yes. I need two rooms for tonight, please," Jackson requested. At Nadine's expression, he worried that he'd offended her somehow.

She tugged at his blazer, and he leaned over so that she could whisper into his ear. "Please don't leave me alone," she begged.

"Okay, if you have a room with two beds, that would be fine, as well," Jackson corrected himself.

The old man looked at Jackson and told him, "You can have whatever you want. We're almost completely empty for tonight."

"Do you know what happened?" Jackson asked, hoping for some answers.

The man shrugged his shoulders. "There just aren't any visitors tonight for some reason."

Jackson worried that the roads were closed off or the nearby towns were already overcome. He was afraid to voice his concerns to the man about the strange people, thinking he would just sound like he was insane. He barely believed it himself, and he'd already lived through it. "Just the one room with two beds, then. Thanks."

The man took Jackson's information and then handed him an old-fashioned metal key with a plastic tag attached to it that had the name of the hotel on it. "It's room 201."

Jackson took the key and then looked for the elevator, which was on the other side of the lobby and near the corridor. Nadine still held onto his blazer as they walked across the small room to the elevator and pressed the button. When they were upstairs, they found the correct door, and he unlocked it before going inside. Checking it out briefly, he saw it was a clean but small room with an en-suite to one side. The décor was like something out of the 1980s in predominantly mauve and teal, but it would do. Then, he said, "I'm going back down to the car. I have an overnight bag. I'll be right back."

He didn't wait for her to protest and hurried out the door and back down to the only slightly more modern lobby.

Looking around carefully outside, he went to his car and opened the back to remove the bag that he'd almost forgotten he had. Suddenly, he wondered what had happened to the view camera, but he assumed he would never see it again. Saddened, he made his way back up to room 201. Nadine started and then let out her breath as he entered.

"Sorry. I forgot about my bag." He set it on one of the beds, then gestured to the en-suite. "Do you want to go take a shower or something? Or at least wash your feet? You don't want those cuts to get infected."

She stood without a word and walked to the bathroom, checking to see that there was soap and shampoo first, then closed the door.

Jackson looked out of the window down to the street, hoping there was nothing to be concerned about. It was very quiet. He hadn't really made up his mind about that, but he opened his bag and searched through it for an undershirt. It might not be large enough for her to sleep in, but he hoped it would be better than the dirty nightdress she was wearing. He found one shirt and then laid it on the other bed for her. While she was still occupied in the shower, he removed his blazer, draped it over the chair, then removed his tie and laid it on top of the blazer. Changing into a tee shirt with some sweatpants, he folded his dirty clothes onto the seat of the chair. Then, he realized he hadn't eaten since earlier in the afternoon as he hadn't expected to be out driving that late and had missed dinner. He wasn't sure if he had anything in his bag, knowing he hadn't planned for that eventuality. Luckily, he found an ancient chocolate chip protein bar from a previous trip but ate it without any enjoyment. It was simply nutrition, and that was all.

It wasn't particularly satisfying, but he set his bag on top of the desk near the chair, and went back to the bed. Pulling the covers back, he slid underneath the blankets, exhausted. He lay there, thinking, trying to solve the mystery of the people he'd seen. What could have happened? Was he safe here? He was extremely tired, but even now, he didn't know if he would be able to sleep.

Eventually, the door opened, and Nadine came out of the bathroom looking cleaner, although her nightdress was still stained and ripped in places. Seeing the undershirt he had laid out for her, she picked it up and took it back into the bathroom. When she came out again, she had the undershirt on, and it was just a bit tight around her curves, but it didn't look uncomfortable. He felt relieved that she wouldn't have to wear the torn garment anymore. She set the grimy nightdress at the foot of the bed, then pulled the covers back. As she lay down, she looked over at him. "Thank you," she said.

"It's not a problem. I can get you some new clothes tomorrow in the town, and then I can take you home if it's safe enough."

"No. I mean, thank you for saving my life. For everything."

He felt uncomfortable receiving the praise. "It's nothing," he responded.

"No one else stopped."

He shook his head. "It's all right. Really. You don't need to thank me for that."

She pursed her lips slightly, then pulled the covers up higher. "I don't know if I want to go home. I don't know if I can ever go back there."

He turned to face her. "Where can I take you instead?"

he asked, concerned.

She sighed. "I don't care."

Her words distressed him slightly, and he didn't know how to comfort her. What she had seen had obviously been very disturbing. "We'll think of something," he said, trying to reassure her. He reached up to turn the lamp off, but she cried out.

"Please, don't turn it off. Please."

He lowered his hand. "No worries. We can leave it on. I'm sorry."

She took a deep breath, then released it shakily. "Thank you."

"It's okay. Really," he reiterated.

She seemed unsure, almost as though she thought he would turn the light out if she weren't looking, but eventually, she settled into the blankets and looked like she might try to sleep.

He wasn't sure if he would be able to relax either and especially not with the light on. But he supposed it would be better to have it on if he had to wake quickly. Sighing, he closed his eyes, hoping he wouldn't have nightmares.

———

CHAPTER

TWO

After a rough and sleepless night, Jackson got out of bed, went to his bag, took out a change of clothes, and then headed to the bathroom for a shower. He hurried through his normal routine, getting out of the tub and drying himself with a towel. Then, he brushed his teeth, washed his face, and trimmed his goatee. He couldn't help but sigh, hoping the nightmare was over, although he had no idea what to do with Nadine. Hopefully, she had family somewhere.

He dressed in another dress shirt and pants but skipped the tie. He could always put it on later, if necessary, he thought. Unfortunately, he hadn't remembered to bring his shoes into the bathroom, but he took the time to put on his socks. Then, he went into the bedroom, hoping he hadn't awakened Nadine. She lay on her bed looking groggy but awake, and he couldn't tell if she'd been asleep.

"I'm sorry if I woke you. I thought I would go get something for breakfast and then find you some clothes if that's all right." The sun was starting to rise, and he went to the window to make sure the coast was clear. However, he didn't see any signs that what had happened the night before was anything other than an isolated incident. He looked up at her to gauge her reaction, but she was just lying there as if accepting that this was just how it was going to be. But he couldn't tell if she was upset or relieved.

"I'll be right back," he said as he put on his shoes. Then, he looked for his car keys and took the hotel key with him as he left the room. The hotel was too small to offer breakfast of any kind, so he walked briskly to the car and nervously started the engine. Driving around the small town, he looked for anything open with a drive-through, but unfortunately, there was no such thing. So, he parked in front of a small diner-style restaurant and went inside to see if they would let him order food to-go.

"Do you do take-out orders?" he asked, sitting at the coffee bar. The woman behind the counter nodded, so he asked for a menu. She left him alone while he reviewed it, wondering what type of foods were acceptable to Nadine. Finally, he ordered an eclectic selection of different foods a la carte (bagels, toast, eggs, hash browns, pastries, and the like) and asked for a couple extra plates if they had any. They did not, the woman said, but she gave him a couple of additional take-out containers instead. Waiting for his order and looking around the restaurant, he saw that it was mostly empty. He didn't think that Nitehurst had as much tourist traffic as Smithton Lake was definitely the bigger of the two, but he would have still expected more people than he'd seen.

Once his food was brought out, he took it gratefully, having already paid. Looking around, he cautiously went out to his car, where he set the food in the passenger seat and drove back to the hotel. When he arrived, he took the unwieldy bags of food out of the car and carried them to the elevator, trying not to let them tip over. As he made it back to the room, he had to set one of the bags on the floor in the hallway to unlock the door, then picked it up again.

Entering the bedroom, he saw Nadine was now up and sitting on her mattress, leaning against the headboard with her pillow propped up behind her. She looked nervous, as if thinking that he would have left her there and never returned, even though he'd left all his other belongings behind.

He took the food over to the small desk and opened the bags. "I didn't know what to get, so I just picked up a small, random assortment. Hopefully, there's something here that you would like." Removing the food containers from the bags, he also took out the two extra containers he'd been given to use as plates. He served some of the food as best as he could with the tiny plastic utensils the restaurant had included in the bags. Then, he turned to look behind him, and Nadine had barely moved. "Are you hungry?" he asked her.

She nodded and slowly stood up, but she seemed wary of approaching the desk. He stepped aside to allow her more room, picking up his clothes off the chair before taking his container and a plastic fork over to his bed so that he could sit to eat. He left the rest of the food on the desk for her to look through. As she came nearer to the desk, she took a small amount of food from a few of the different containers and then glanced at him like she was afraid of offending him somehow. Then, she took her container to her bed and scooted herself back to the far side, away from the edge.

"Is everything okay?" he asked.

She shrugged, but she still looked scared.

"Did I do something?"

She shook her head.

"So, what happened? Did you have a nightmare?" he thought aloud.

She nodded.

"Was it about me?"

Looking like she was going to cry, she nodded.

"Okay, but it was just a dream. Try to relax. Everything will be fine." He hoped that was true. He ate slowly, thinking. Unfortunately, he hadn't seen any clothing stores except one resale shop near the hotel. But he thought he would go there to get Nadine something decent to wear as he knew she couldn't wear a torn nightdress in case they had to go anywhere else.

Ideally, of course, he hoped the ordeal was over.

When he looked up again, Nadine was eating. She picked at the food as if she were not really interested, but she did manage to finish her plate. Then, she set the empty container aside, pulling a blanket over her as she pulled her legs up and almost curled into a ball.

"I'm sorry things turned out the way they did." He finished his food, then stood up, startling her. "I'm going to go find you something decent to wear. You can't go out in public with that," he told her, pointing to her dirty garment. "I'll try to get something you might actually want to wear. Just let me know what you want."

She didn't answer but just pointed at the dress.

"Dresses?" he asked. She nodded. "Okay." He picked it up and looked at the tag for the size, and then departed. This was turning out to be more difficult than it should have been, he thought. He knew she was traumatized, but he felt like he was trying to decipher a hidden code to figure out what she wanted. It didn't help that he had no idea how to buy clothes for women, either. Obviously, he'd bought clothes for his ex, but that had been after he had known her for a long time.

Walking to the store, he checked to be sure it was open before going inside. There were hardly any patrons, and he didn't know if it were just because it was still early in the day or because the town was somewhat deserted. Looking around to orient himself, he saw that the dresses were in a section by themselves. He found her size and tried to guess what she might like, but of course, he really had no clue. Trying to gauge what might be comfortable in addition to being somewhat attractive, he didn't know what she might think was pretty as opposed to what he might like for her. So again, he picked up a somewhat random selection. Additionally, he picked up a couple of large tee shirts for her to sleep in and a pair of sandals. He didn't see anywhere he could buy undergarments, but he was determined that he would take her somewhere later so that she could choose those for herself.

When he completed the purchase, he walked back to the hotel, carefully looking around him but not seeing any other people around at all. It was unnerving. Going back up to the room, he looked around for Nadine. She was still curled under the blankets as if she'd tried to sleep.

"Hope I didn't wake you," he apologized, entering the room.

She sat up blearily and wiped her hair out of her eyes as he set the bag down for her to go through. A little timidly, she took it off the end of the bed and pulled all of the items out, noticing that he'd bought her four dresses and two tee shirts and a pair of sandals. She sat there looking at them, even setting her hand on a couple of them as if admiring the fabric or pattern, although she had yet to smile.

"Are these okay? I don't know if they'll let me take them back. I'm sorry. I can go back and ask."

She shook her head, picking up one of the dresses. "Thank you." Then she stood and wiped her eyes again before going into the bathroom for some privacy.

He sighed. He had no idea if he was upsetting her or if he was making her even slightly happy. Without any input, he didn't know what she wanted him to do, and he hoped he could find somewhere for her to stay. Not knowing if he could go home or not, he wanted to try, and he doubted she would want to go that far with him. Obviously, he would feel awkward taking her, anyway. Then, he wondered if he could convince his mother or someone to look after her, at least temporarily.

Nadine opened the door to the bathroom and stood in the doorway wearing a plain red tank dress. She wiped her eyes yet again and said, "Thank you." Then, she sat down and started to fold the other clothes into the bag they had come in. He then realized that she had no hairbrush, toothpaste or toothbrush, deodorant, or any such things. Knowing he would have to stop again, he sighed to himself. He also contemplated buying her an inexpensive overnight bag. Even if she found somewhere to stay, it would be difficult to go far with just a cheap plastic bag that might rip and leave her with nothing.

"Do you want to go out with me later? We need to pick up some toiletries for you and maybe some other things. I just don't know what you would want."

Looking slightly confused but not as scared this time, she nodded.

"Okay. Let's take all of this down to the car, and then we can stop somewhere on the way. Is there any food left?"

She nodded again.

"Maybe see what things will keep, and we'll take those with us? See what you think, and I'll pack my bag." Jackson went to his bag and repacked it while Nadine checked the food containers. They consolidated everything into as few bags as possible, managing to get the food that was easiest to transport and store into one container and bag, and he squeezed her clothes into his overnight bag with his own things for the time being.

They took their bags downstairs to the lobby, where Jackson paid for the room and returned the key. Then, they cautiously went out into the sunshine. It was getting hot already, but he didn't see anyone on the streets or otherwise. Relieved, he put his overnight bag into the car's trunk, then they both got into the front. Nadine had the bag with the food and set it on the floor in the back of the car. Driving away, he looked for the nearest drugstore or supermarket. However, it wasn't until he was on the way back to the main road that he saw a store that looked almost like a CVS Pharmacy, and he parked outside.

"Let's do this quickly, all right? I'll see if I can get some medical supplies for your cuts, and you can pick up whatever you might want for...erm...undergarments and the like. If you want a toothbrush and things like that, pick those up, too, okay?" He got a nod. "Let's go."

They hurried inside, and he was still puzzled that there were no patrons and only a couple of employees were present. He decided to worry about it later, although it was still unsettling. Taking a shopping handcart, he went straight for the first aid section and picked up as much as he thought they might need for a few days, just in case. Next, he found a beach bag, instead of a suitcase or overnight bag but thought it would accomplish the task. Then, he looked around for Nadine. He found her looking at hairbrushes, but she already had some other items with her. He took some of them from her and set them in the cart so she would have her hands free. She handed him her last choices as they headed for the register. Before he paid, he checked to make sure she had everything she might need and suggested she pick up a few things that she had missed, like facial moisturizer, body lotion, and a razor. She ran to get them and then rushed back.

When he had paid, and the items were bagged, he

urged her out to the car, setting the bags in the back seat, although she kept the one with the hairbrush and lip balm. Then, he got into the driver's seat and waited for her to buckle her seat belt.

"What do you want to do? I think we need to get away from here. It's still odd, you know?" Jackson asked.

She nodded.

"Okay, so where do you want to go, though? I'll probably head to Spring Haven for now, but I can drop you off anywhere."

She took a deep breath. "I don't have anywhere to go. I'm not from here."

He had noticed a bit of an accent, but she spoke so little that he couldn't be sure. "Okay, so we'll just go to Spring Haven for now, all right? We'll figure something out." He turned on the ignition and pulled out of the parking space. Then, he turned the car toward the main road out of town and drove toward Spring Haven.

———

The road was virtually empty as they left. They hardly saw any people in the town or driving away, and Jackson regretted that he hadn't spoken to the clerk at the drugstore to see if he might have had an idea what had happened, although he was still paranoid about sounding crazy. But he had been too anxious to leave. He hoped that wasn't a mistake, but there wasn't anything to do about it now. Maybe the whole disaster was over already anyway, and there was nothing more to worry about.

Jackson looked around for someplace to pick up lunch, but there weren't many restaurants as the road was very rural and lined mostly by rows of trees. The few restaurants that were there looked completely unoccupied. As an afterthought, he wished now that he'd picked up some snacks while they were at the store.

Eventually, they were out of the Nitehurst area and away from the nearby farms, as well. It was just an empty road surrounded by towering pine trees as far as he could see. He knew they still had a few hours of driving to go, however.

"What's in the food bag?" he asked Nadine, then pointed toward the back seat with his thumb.

She reached through to the back where the bags were left, and she found the one with the food in it on the floor where she'd set it down. Then, she pulled it through to the front and looked inside. Opening the container, she then showed it to Jackson. It was mostly just toast, a bagel, and four pastries.

"Okay, just hand me anything. I'm hungry." He held out a hand, and she gave him a slice of lightly buttered toast.

Nadine picked out the asiago cheese bagel and nibbled at it while Jackson ate the toast as quickly as he could manage while driving. Finishing the bagel, Nadine put the food bag down on the floor in the back of the car again. Then, she took out the hairbrush she'd kept and brushed out her hair. It was straight and just past shoulder-length and extremely tangled after her ordeal the night before. It took a while for her to work the knots out. Next, she put the brush back in the bag and picked up the lip balm, opening it and applying some of it to her lips before setting it back in the bag. Then she stared out the side window and watched the line of trees pass by as they drove as if lost in thought.

Jackson wanted to start a conversation with her, but she was resistant to questioning of any sort. He wondered if she spoke English very well, but she seemed to understand him, so maybe that wasn't it. It was difficult to stay awake staring at the road, and he considered turning on the radio for the local news but decided he would wait until they got closer to Spring Haven. The signal wasn't strong enough that far away anyway. He regretted that he'd never subscribed to satellite radio, although there wasn't a guarantee that any of the stations were broadcasting regardless.

By dinner time, they had not found a restaurant, and the town was still about an hour away. He debated eating more of their food from that morning or trying to wait, but he had eaten so little that he didn't think he could make it. In the end, he took a pastry she gave him, something like a cheese Danish, and ate that as he drove, hoping it would hold him off until they reached their destination. However, it barely filled him up, and he already wanted another one. But he didn't want to eat too much of their food in case they needed it later. So, he tried to keep an eye out as he drove for any place where they could pick up cooked food.

He stopped once at a gas station to fill up the car's fuel tank. But unfortunately, the convenience store attached to it was closed. Concerned, he got back in the car and drove away. He didn't know what to do if they couldn't find any place that was open. However, Spring Haven was a large town, and he hoped they would find something there upon arrival.

When the sun started to go down, Nadine seemed edgy. He looked around, but he didn't see anything worrisome. Chalking it up to trauma, he kept going. He thought he could see more people now, so maybe they were going in the right direction. Nadine looked close to panic. They had almost reached the town, and they were still on the outskirts, but he hoped there would be someplace nearby to eat. However, although some of the houses looked occupied, he didn't see any signs that any of the businesses were open. As they got closer to Spring Haven, he saw more people wandering the streets up ahead, and it seemed odd after being in an almost empty Nitehurst earlier in the day.

Unfortunately, the closer he got to the town, he could see that these were not ordinary people but the strange people he'd seen around Smithton Lake. Their appearance had changed, however. Their skin had darkened slightly as if necrosis were taking over, and more of the wounds were oozing or bleeding. They still moved in an almost mechanical manner that didn't look human at all, but he couldn't quite place why. A chill went down his spine at seeing them, and he feared that he had made a deadly mistake by going there.

Nadine had clenched her seat in her hands in terror, and she was now trying to get his attention by grabbing his shirt. "No, no, no," he protested to himself as he hit the gas pedal harder and headed for the highway. He swerved around the people as they tried to come after his car. Then, he turned at the next intersection and saw more of the same. He tried not to curse but kept going, swerving and dodging, until he reached the highway. Gunning the engine on the on-ramp, he sped away from the town.

There were still some of the strange people scattered around the highway. However, they seemed to be mostly lined up on the sides of the road, waiting for him to pass, and then they would lunge at the car. Nadine screamed as one of them hit the window without breaking it, leaving a smear of red and yellow on the glass. The stranger fell back in the rearview mirror as Jackson sped up slightly, trying to escape. Obviously, he didn't want to damage his only means of transportation, so he tried to keep to the center line. He didn't see any other escaping vehicles, but he didn't want to risk an accident either, so he didn't go as quickly as he would have liked. But he kept driving, wondering how far he would have to go to find a safe place. What was going on? How could this have happened?

He reached a junction and decided to head for the smaller town rather than the larger one, remembering that there weren't any of the strangers in Nitehurst, but they had been present in considerable numbers in Smithton Lake. Nervously, he hoped his gamble would pay off, knowing it would be a long way to another larger town if he stopped in Kinsing Valley. But he didn't want to chance going the other way.

It wasn't a wide highway, and it turned into another two-lane road after the junction. He could see some of the strangers mobbing something or someone to the side of the road, but he didn't stop to see what they were doing. Nadine was crying again.

Driving further on, the number of strangers decreased again, but they seemed to be more aggressive somehow. They'd been mostly ambling and had lunged at cars, but it seemed to be almost an afterthought before. Now, it seemed that their lunging was more purposeful. He also hadn't seen the mobbing behavior before either, which was unsettling, thinking that the strangers could and would change with time. What was next? Would it be worse than now?

He kept driving, and soon, but not soon enough, they were between towns, and there were few, if any, of the strangers. Although he wanted to sigh in relief, he wasn't sure

it was over. They'd never eaten dinner, and he wasn't sure
he would find a restaurant or store out there in the relative
wilderness, so he asked Nadine to give him another pastry.
There wasn't much left, so Nadine took one, also. That only
left one more. There was nothing else.

———————

When they arrived in Kinsing Valley that evening, Jackson
again pulled the car off the main road and onto the smaller,
narrower streets, hoping to avoid notice. The town looked
almost deserted, with darkened and empty buildings, but he
didn't want to take any chances. A few streetlights seemed to be
functioning and spilled golden light onto the pavement below
them. He turned the vehicle lights off and slowed, stopping
outside another quaint hotel. There was a convenience store
next door, and he thought they should stop before moving
on. The lights were on, so he hoped that meant it was open for
business. Nadine and he got out of the car and walked to the
store, feeling a warm breeze blow past them, carrying a hint
of uneasiness with it as if there were the ghosts of the dead
watching them. Jackson cautiously opened the door, hearing
a bell above it, and Nadine almost bolted, but he held on to
her arm and guided her inside. Quickly, they picked up a few
bags of chips, some more pastries, and some soup. He found
some deli sandwiches, and he picked out two, then they went
to check out. However, there wasn't a store clerk anywhere to
be seen, and he started to get worried. He looked behind him
and back through the store. Nothing. Then, he looked out the
front door. Nothing there, either. But with the lights on in the
store, it was difficult to see out the windows.

Waiting a little longer, he could see that Nadine was
getting anxious. He wanted to leave but didn't want to leave

their groceries behind. "Hello?" he called out finally. Nadine had her arm around his, and he could feel her trembling. "Is anyone there?"

A young man came out of the back of the store, peeking his head out first and then walking to the register. "I'm sorry to keep you waiting. It's been slow, and I didn't expect to see anyone," the man said. He started to ring up their merchandise and bag it.

"Do you know what's been going on the past two nights?" Jackson asked him.

"What? No. I haven't heard anything. The TV is out, and so is the radio."

Well, that ruined Jackson's plan. "Have you seen anything?"

The man considered Jackson's words. "Well, it's just been quiet around here. No one has been out and about."

"Is that unusual?"

"Yes. For this time of year, we're usually pretty busy."

Jackson was still puzzled. He didn't understand what was happening and wondered if anyone else did either. The man finished ringing them up, and Jackson paid, then thanked the man, wanting to warn him to leave but thinking he wouldn't believe him or do what he asked anyway. It wasn't as though it sounded believable to him, either.

"Maybe you should just close the store and go home for the night. It doesn't seem safe to be here by yourself," Jackson suggested anyway.

"Nah. It's fine. I don't want to lose any time from my paycheck. I'll be okay," the man insisted.

"I still think you should go home. Something is wrong," Jackson tried to warn the man.

The clerk shook his head as if to shake off any doubts. "I'm sure it will be back to normal tomorrow," he said.

Reluctantly, Jackson left and took the bags to the car, helping Nadine pack everything into as few bags as possible. Then, they carried their two overnight bags (or his overnight bag and Nadine's beach bag) and a couple of bags of food to the hotel to see if they could get a room.

At the reception desk, there was still no one present, and Jackson made sure to ring the bell resting on the counter. It took some time, but eventually, an older brunette woman came out looking a bit confused, but she smiled warmly when she saw that she had visitors. "How can I help you? Do you need a room for tonight?"

"With two beds, please," Jackson replied.

She looked at the computer and lamented, "Our system seems to be down. I can take your information on paper if that's okay with you."

The woman slid a form across the desk to him, and he filled out the paperwork and handed it back. She looked through the available keys and handed him one. "It's room 315."

"Thank you," he replied. Nadine and he went across the lobby to the elevator and up to the third floor. It was the top floor of that hotel, so he hoped it would be safer from any intruders. Jackson opened the door to the room and turned on the light. It wasn't a large room, but it was slightly larger than the previous one and decorated in an almost Old-World style. It also boasted a small table with two chairs in addition to the beds, nightstand, and TV armoire. He checked the en-suite and saw that there were still bottles of shampoo and some soap, as well as plenty of towels. The paper products were stocked recently, too.

He returned to the bedroom, where Nadine was already heating some noodles in the microwave. Setting his bag on one of the beds, he sat down heavily, then removed his shoes. He wanted to get more comfortable after being in the car for so long, but he realized he didn't want to fall asleep in his current outfit. So, he stood up again and took some sleep clothes out of his bag. Taking them into the bathroom, he changed, then folded up his old clothes and carried them back to the bedroom.

By then, Nadine was eating, sitting on one of the beds, but there was something else in the microwave. "Is that mine?" he asked her, and she nodded. "Thank you."

He put the clothes back in his overnight bag and sat on the bed he'd sat down on previously. Sighing, he put his feet up and leaned back against the headboard, closing his eyes. However, almost as soon as he'd done so, the microwave beeped, and he stood to take his food out of it. Stirring the noodles, he remembered to grab the remote off the top of the armoire before sitting down again.

Then, he turned on the TV to hopefully catch the news, but he only saw the off-air signals as he flipped the channels, remembering the store clerk's words about the media being out. Disappointed, he turned it off again and set down the remote. Again, he stirred the noodles and looked up at Nadine. She was still eating but had a vacant expression, and she had pulled her legs up next to her almost defensively.

"Are you all right?" he asked her.

She seemed to snap out of her trance, and she nodded.

"What happened?"

She gave him a questioning look.

"They weren't just 'in the house,' were they? What happened?"

She shook her head. "No."

"No, you won't tell me, or no, they weren't just 'in the house'?"

Setting the noodles on the nightstand, she wrapped her arms around herself and huddled in the corner.

"Look. I know there's more to it than that."

Her breathing turned more ragged, and a few tears escaped before she could wipe them away. "I don't want to think about it."

"I'm not accusing you of anything. I just think it would help if I knew more about what's going on." He set his noodles on his side of the nightstand, ready to listen. "So, what happened?"

She sighed at last. "It was my boyfriend's house. I came here to live with him. I tried to go to bed, but I heard the door. We'd just argued earlier, so I was scared. I thought he was leaving. I heard what sounded like fighting, and I went into the main part of the house. Those people were there. I saw… they killed my boyfriend. Right in front of me…they broke his neck and…I don't want to say more." She was sobbing fully by the time she finished her short story.

"I'm sorry. I just…we need to know what's happening. We can't do anything without knowing more."

"I'm sorry," she cried.

"No. I'm sorry. I didn't want to upset you. I just thought it might help us figure out what to do. What do they want? You know?"

She shook her head. "I don't know what they want. I don't know if they want anything. Just to kill us all."

"They chased you?"

She nodded.

"I'll do what I can, but I don't know how long we'll be safe here, and I don't know where we can go from here." He sighed. Then, he picked up his noodles and started eating again. "So, you don't know anyone in the area at all?"

"No. I'm from France." As if that explained everything.

"Okay." Trying not to draw out the word, he thought some more. "I'm not from here, either. I live in Moorston Park, but we've turned away from it now. I don't know where else to go."

She was still crying. "You didn't have to stop."

"What? What do you mean?"

"You didn't have to stop. You could have left me there."

"What? Of course, I had to stop. Where's this coming from?" Jackson set his food down again.

She couldn't answer. She just cried harder and shook her head at him.

"There's nothing you could have done. It's all right. None of this is your fault. I would be in this mess if I were on my own, too," he insisted.

She didn't stop sobbing and still looked a little like she was afraid of him.

"What's wrong? Did I do something?" he asked her.

She shook her head again. Still weeping. Still upset.

"What can I do, then? How can I fix something if I don't know what the problem is?"

She wiped her eyes. "I don't want to be on my own. I'm sorry. Just don't leave me behind."

"Have I ever said I would do that?"

"No, but you get mad at me sometimes." She was sniffling and trying to talk at the same time.

"When? When have I been mad at you?"

"Now."

He rolled his eyes. "I'm not mad. I'm frustrated. There's a difference. And I'm not upset with you. I just don't know what to do. And yeah, I'm a bit scared, too, although I didn't want to admit it."

She wiped her eyes again.

Jackson stood up and went to the bathroom, then removed the box of tissues from its holder and brought it to her. She almost seemed to recoil from him at first, but she accepted the tissues almost timidly.

"Besides," he continued, "I'm really just frustrated at not having any answers. It would be easier if I did."

She blew her nose lightly, then took another tissue. "I'm sorry."

"For what?"

"That I don't know any more."

He sighed again. "That's not it. That's not what I'm saying. It's just that I don't know anything about you, and you don't speak to me half the time. At least, if you did, it might be more like I have help to sort this out, you know?"

She sobbed into the tissue and wiped her eyes.

"It's not a criticism. It's just a suggestion. If you don't think you can talk, it's fine. But, if it concerns you, then I would appreciate it if you would try." He tried to speak as softly and non-threateningly as he could as he returned to his previous position on his bed.

She took out another tissue.

"I'll tell you some more about myself if you want.

Would that help?" Jackson sat up slightly, but he scooted back away from the edge of the bed so that he would hopefully look less intimidating. "What do you want to know?"

Nadine shook her head, trying to stop crying, but she blew her nose again, and the sobbing seemed to have eased partly.

"It's all right. You can ask anything. I promise to tell the truth." He tried to smile.

She tried to smile back, but she ended up just wiping her eyes and blowing her nose again. Taking some deep breaths to calm herself, her breathing became more normal, and the tears slowed. "I'll be okay. I'm sorry I've been so much trouble."

"Just stop apologizing over it. It's all right. I've been trouble, too." He grinned.

She shook her head. "No, you haven't."

"I haven't been able to do what I wanted yet, though, have I? I wanted to get somewhere safe and get some real food. And…." She looked like she was trying to determine if he was joking. "Okay, so can I ask you something then?"

She nodded.

"What's your last name?"

Puzzled, she answered, "Dardenne."

"Okay, so mine's Riley." He smiled. "What about your favorite color?"

"Purple," she replied, still looking confused.

"Mine's grey. Hmm. What about…er…music? What sort of music do you usually listen to?"

"I don't know."

Jackson thought a moment. "I'm usually on the rock side, but I do listen to other styles of music. I'm guessing you're a polka sort of girl."

She made a sound almost as if she'd tried to laugh. "No. It's usually pop or rock."

He realized he hadn't finished his noodles and picked them up again. "Family?" he asked before taking another rather bland bite. There was a sauce of some sort, but it mostly just tasted salty.

"No. Just my parents in France."

"I've got my parents still, but they've split up. I don't get to see them very often, though." He sounded somewhat sad. Instead of dwelling on it, he changed the subject. "Where in France?"

"What?"

"Where are you from?" He finished the noodles and set the empty container down. However, when he looked at hers, he saw that she had barely started eating them. "You can finish that if you want."

She looked down as if noticing them for the first time, then picked the container up and started eating again. "I'm from Marseilles, but I was attending university in Paris."

"A city girl."

She nodded, but she didn't comment. Then, she looked at him expectantly.

"Oh. Well, I was born in New York, but I lived in England and then Ireland for a while. But really, I've lived all over and traveled a lot. I'm not sure I really know where I'm from exactly."

"What do you do for a living?" she asked. It was her first time asking him a question.

"I'm a freelance photographer. I was leaving a job when all of this happened. I had to leave one of my cameras behind." He sighed. "What about you? What did you do?"

"In Paris, I was studying law. I met David one day at lunch, and that was it. He was a tourist in Paris. We ate lunch and dinner together every day while he was there. When he left to go home, we wrote to each other for a long time and talked on the phone nearly every day. But eventually, I left Paris to live with him in Smithton Lake."

She seemed to get upset again, and he wished he hadn't asked. "I'm sorry. I didn't know it would be so hard to speak about," he said.

She finished her noodles and sat back. "I wish this hadn't happened."

"Me, too."

Suddenly, he heard a thumping noise in the hallway, thinking that some other guests had arrived, but he decided it was better to be safe than sorry. Going to the peephole as quietly as he could, he looked out. But it was dark in the hallway, and he had trouble making out the other figures that were there, although they seemed to be moving away from the door. He turned to her and put his finger to his lips, asking her to stay silent. He continued to watch, but there was nothing for several minutes. Then, he gave up and went to sit down. But he didn't remember the hallway being that dark before. Again, he stood and returned to the door, looking out and trying to see what might have happened. However, there were no changes, and it was quiet.

"Maybe we should try to sleep. We might have to leave tomorrow. We should be prepared, you know?"

She nodded. "Okay." Nervously.

Nadine finally went to the bathroom to change into one of the tee shirts that Jackson had bought her and to clean her injuries with antiseptic. Then, she went back to the bed and lay down, curling under the blankets and trying to relax.

He left the light on, but neither of them could sleep that night.

———

CHAPTER

THREE

When the sunrays started to break through the window, Jackson climbed out of bed and picked out some clothes for the day, then went into the bathroom to take a shower. Shampooing his hair, he couldn't help but face the day with some trepidation. He was worried that something had taken place during the night. What would happen now? Where could they go? Where was safe? Turning the water off, he started to dry himself with a towel. Then, he took the time to brush his teeth and wash his face afterward, and to trim his goatee. He dressed in his usual dress shirt and slacks, then combed his short, brown hair back. Wrapping up his routine quickly, he left the towel behind, off to one side of the counter and out of the way so that Nadine could take a shower if she wanted.

When he entered the bedroom, however, it appeared that she'd finally dozed. He wanted to get breakfast, but he wasn't sure if the hotel served one as he hadn't seen much of a lobby when he'd been downstairs. Instead, he found the bag they'd picked up from the small store the day before. Finding a pastry, he opened the wrapper as he sat down at the table. Then, he ate it slowly, trying not to rush, as he didn't yet know what the plan was going to be for that day.

Suddenly, he remembered that he still had his phone with him, but it had been in his overnight bag when he'd gone into the lab to shoot the photos, which seemed like years ago now. Going to his bag, he hunted around until he found it, then sat down again. When he pulled up the news, though, he saw that it was all a couple of days old. There wasn't anything new, there wasn't a wi-fi signal at all, and the phone was almost dead. Frustrated, he wished he could find out what was happening. Perhaps it wasn't just the radio and television stations that were down. Perhaps it was all media. That was a frightening thought, as he worried that the disaster wasn't just a local event. Then, he thought he should check on his family, the few he had, and he sent messages to a couple of them. However, it soon became clear that the messages weren't getting through, or something had happened as there was no answer, even after several minutes, which was unusual.

He heard Nadine stir, and he looked over to make sure she didn't need anything. She seemed slightly disoriented at being in the strange room, but she sat up and wiped her eyes, seeing the empty bed across from her and then finding him sitting at the table. She took a deep breath and then joined him. Taking out another pastry from the bag, she opened it and nibbled on it like she was only partially interested. As usual, she seemed distracted and sad. At that point, he knew there was still something she wasn't telling him, and it was bothering her immensely.

"Are you all right?" he asked her.

She looked up at him. "I don't know. I'm still worried."

"Me, too," he replied. "But that's not what I meant."

"What did you mean, then?"

He sighed. "Look. I know it must have been terrifying. And I apologize. But I feel like there's something important that you're not telling me about the night that your boyfriend was killed. Whatever it is, I know you can't forget it, but I don't know if it's something I need to know or not."

"It's not," she answered. "It was horrific, but it's not something that's relevant. It's just the manner in which he was killed. I can't get the image out of my head." Her voice broke on the last three words.

"Okay. Never mind. I'm sorry. I'm just worried that it

might be important somehow. Does it speak to what they're after or what they intend to do?"

"Yes, but only partly. I just think they're evil and have no remorse at all. They don't seem human." She was trying to regain control of her emotions.

"I can gather that much," he responded. "They don't move the same. There's something wrong about them. But what's going on? Where did they come from? Can we reason with them?"

"No. Absolutely not. We need to avoid them at all costs." About that, she was adamant.

"But why?"

She looked like she was trying to decide how much to tell him. "They just want us dead. I don't know why."

"How do you know?"

She shook her head. "It was...they seemed to...when they killed him, they showed no emotion at all. It was like they were just doing what they were supposed to do."

He tried to process what she had told him. Was this important? He felt like there was something he should be able to figure out. "Do they seem to...I don't know...have normal abilities? Can they figure things out?"

"I don't know. I didn't wait to see."

"Do you think we're safe here?"

Looking doubtful, she shook her head again. "Probably not."

He remembered the thumping sounds outside their door the night before, and he was afraid to look out, but he got up and went to the peephole again. There was no sign that there had been anything amiss, but it was hard to tell with the darkness. It still seemed much dimmer than on their arrival, but that was all he could tell through the tiny aperture.

"Maybe we should pack, just in case," he told her. He went into the bathroom, retrieved his toiletries, then took them back to his bag.

She quickly finished her pastry and took a dress and some undergarments out of her bag. Then, she went into the bathroom for privacy. He heard the shower start and tried to get everything else together from the night before. Luckily, they hadn't really unpacked, so he just put his sleep clothes in his bag and threw the empty food containers into the trash. He made sure the grocery bag was still together. Then, he sat on the bed, still afraid to open the door.

When the shower stopped, he knew she still had a short hygiene routine that she had to complete, along with taking care of her injuries, so he lay back and tried to close his eyes briefly. He heard the sink turn on and heard her brushing her teeth. Then, suddenly she was out of the bathroom and staring at him like she'd been speaking for a while, looking almost panicked.

"What?" he said, confused. Then he sat up and realized that he must have dozed off. "Sorry." He got out of the bed and wiped his face with his hands, then went to the window and looked out, but everything looked as still and deserted as the day before.

Turning away from the window, he looked at Nadine. "What do you think? Do you want to stay here?"

She looked torn. "I don't know."

He crossed the room and looked out the peephole again, still seeing nothing. Annoyed that the doors were set slightly back from the walls, limiting his view, he took a deep breath, then opened the door as quietly and carefully as he could manage. Once he'd looked up and down the hallway, he rushed back into the room.

"Get your bag. We're leaving now," he told her urgently. Picking up his bag and the grocery bag, he waited for her to grab hers. Then, they both went to the door. He paused at the threshold and made a decision. "Close your eyes," he strongly suggested.

She looked alarmed. "What? Why?"

"You don't want to see. Close your eyes. I'll lead you down the hallway. Please."

Frightened, she closed her eyes, and he led her carefully down the hallway. Jackson feared that they weren't alone in the hotel anymore. He tried to avoid any obstacles, but it was nearly impossible. There had been people in the hallway the night before, but they had been ripped apart. Limbs, decapitated torsos, and even heads scattered the length of the hallway. However, the stench alone was enough to make him want to get away. The strong odor of copper and feces assailed his senses, and he fought back his gag response as he led her to the elevator, trying to keep her from stepping on any body parts as she walked. But it was unavoidable. When they reached the elevator, he pressed the button, and they waited. When the doors opened, he was trying not to panic. There was still more blood in the carriage. "Don't open your eyes yet," he advised her. She was trying not to cry. "Keep them closed."

When the carriage reached ground level, he quickly led her out into the lobby. Checking to see that they were still unobserved, they ran across the parking lot and out to his parked vehicle. There was nothing around it, so he told her, "Open your eyes and get in the car."

She hurried to comply. He'd started the ignition almost before her door was closed, then he drove away while simultaneously securing his seatbelt. He watched her struggle with hers before finally hearing the click. Then, he turned down the main road and didn't know which way to go. Debating it briefly, he only knew he couldn't return to Spring Haven. In the end, he decided to continue away from it and toward more of the smaller towns. He sped away and raced down the road.

"What happened?" Nadine asked. She was breathing heavily from fear, and he could tell she was about to start crying again.

"I have a feeling you already know," he answered.

She looked shocked and stared at him. "No. No, no, no."

"I'm sorry, but I don't know if anyone survived there. I think we're very lucky we had sturdy locks on the door."

The tears finally started to come down. "What can we do? How can we stop them?"

He shook his head. "I wish I knew."

Nadine opened a small bag of potato chips and handed them to Jackson. Again, there was no place to eat lunch, so he drove through the town nearest Kinsing Valley without stopping. He didn't think he could make it far with just snacks, but he didn't know where to go to obtain anything else. Looking to the sides of the road as he drove, he watched for the strange people and wondered how to avoid them. He hadn't yet seen any during the day, but he didn't think that was necessarily indicative of how the people behaved. They'd changed before. He just wanted Nadine and himself to be safe. But was there any place safe now? He'd hoped they would be safer in the smaller towns, but that didn't seem to be the case after the night before.

He ate the chips slowly, more vigilant than during the previous day. As it seemed the strangers could change their behavior, he was wary at that point. What if the next town started out empty, and the people showed up later as they did the night before? What could he and Nadine do? What if the people were present from the start? Crumpling the bag as he finished it, he wondered what they would do about dinner, too. He didn't want to rely on their supplies if they didn't have to. Also, he worried about paying for any more supplies. Perhaps he should get some actual currency in case the computer systems went down. However, he also feared what would happen if this continued much longer. Would everyone end up looting for supplies and food? He didn't want to stoop to that level, but how would he feel when he was hungry, and there were no open shops or restaurants to be found?

"Could you hand me a water, please?" Jackson asked Nadine. They only had a few drinks, and he wished they would have been able to restock those again before leaving Kinsing Valley.

She handed him the drink and took the wadded-up chip bag to put into the makeshift trash. Having eaten some chips, also, she already had a bottle of water in the cup holder next to the passenger door.

"Thank you," he told her. He tried to open it with his teeth and drive with one hand, but the car swerved slightly.

Nadine took the bottle back and opened it, then returned it to him. "Sorry."

"No worries," he replied, trying not to show how concerned he really was. He couldn't get the image of the hotel hallway out of his mind. Obviously, he tried to think of just about anything else, but it was nearly impossible. Now, he understood why Nadine was so traumatized if she'd seen someone whom she loved being murdered that way first-hand. He was terrified of running into the strangers again himself.

They passed a roadway sign stating that Bridgeford was next. He hoped it would be safe for a few days at least, but he knew he couldn't let his guard down at all. It looked as if they would reach the town around dinnertime. The road was somewhat narrow and winding, and he didn't want to drive too quickly through that section. He kept close to the speed limit, thinking it was better to reach the town later in the evening and get there safely. However, he couldn't help being anxious about being out driving late at night.

Nadine sat silently most of the time. He was torn between bothering her and trying to take her mind off past trauma and letting her come to terms with it on her own. With no experience at that sort of thing, he didn't know which was better. She stared out the windows, but always nervously.

Later that afternoon, he saw a gas station ahead and pulled over to refuel. The tank wasn't empty, but he didn't want to count on finding another one later when he really needed it. He put the nozzle into the tank and started filling it, then went inside the store to use the ATM. There didn't appear to be anyone there, and the store was dim, but he quickly took as many bottles of water as he could carry, and took them to the register, then tried to take some money out of the ATM. The screen was black, however, and nothing he did would bring up the start screen. Giving up, he went back to the register and waited for several minutes, but he could see Nadine's expression out the window. She had taken the nozzle out for him and replaced it on the pump, but she looked near panic.

"Hello, hello?" Jackson called out. He waited a little longer, but he didn't want to leave Nadine alone too long. Finally, he walked toward the back of the store and looked for the office. "Hello?" Feeling the hairs on the back of his neck and his arms start to stand up, he looked toward the open door in the back. The familiar smell of copper and decomposition was strong, and he could see blood on the floor before he got close. Cautiously, he backed away, hoping the person or persons responsible were no longer present. He didn't bother to check to see if there was a body, knowing without looking for it that no one could survive that amount of blood loss. Scrambling, he hurried back to the register, bagged the water, and then ran toward the car.

He passed the bags to Nadine through her window, then something occurred to him, and he ran back toward the store. She was calling him to come back, but he leapt behind the counter and searched around underneath the register. There, he found a handgun and a few bullets. He wasn't sure how long that would last if they were surrounded, but he hoped it would be enough to protect them that night at least. Looking behind him as he sprinted again for the car, he then started the ignition and quickly fastened his seat belt as he drove away.

Nadine looked alarmed at him as he tried to stow the gun in the glove compartment. "Where did you get that? Did you just rob that store?" she asked, terrified.

He looked over at her, then back at the road. "Of course not. What would give you that idea?" Then, he saw the gun in his hand and remembered running from the store. "Oh. Well, I don't think the owner cares that I took the water or that gun. He wasn't available, and the systems were down."

"Then why were you running?" she asked.

"Because…I know where the owner was. He was in the office, and I didn't want to look more closely, all right?" He pleaded with her with his voice to not ask any more questions as he sat up straight to look at the road.

She seemed to pick up on it, and she dropped the subject. "Okay. Never mind."

"I don't know when we'll be able to stop. Try to minimize how much water you drink."

She had been about to take a sip but put the bottle back in the cup holder. "I didn't get to use the restroom at the gas station."

"Me, neither. I wouldn't complain about that."

She looked frustrated. "No, I *needed* to use it."

He sighed. "I don't know what to do about that. I did, too. I can pull over, but you'll have to stay near the car."

She sighed. "Okay. I really have to go."

Quickly, he pulled the car off the road and close to a copse of trees. "Stay here." He got out of the car and hurried over to the trees to make sure there was nothing hidden there, and then he signaled Nadine as he walked back to the car. "Hurry. I don't want to stay in one place too long."

She hurried away from the car as he reached it, and he kept an eye out for anything suspicious near the roadway. When she ran back to the car, he decided to take a turn and walked back to the trees. He heard her sound the horn as he finished relieving himself, and he rushed to see what she had seen. When he could see the car, he saw her pointing back in the direction they had just come from. Looking over as he ran back to the car, he could see figures in the distance. Alarmed, he started to sprint and made it to the driver's seat right as he saw the figures nearing the car. He slammed the door and barely checked to make sure that Nadine's door was closed, as well, before gunning the engine.

Looking in the rear-view mirror to make sure they were safely away, he saw that there was a glint of something like metal underneath the rotting skin of the strange people in the glow of the taillights. Their skin was now peeling and decaying worse than before. But that didn't make any sense, did it? Who were those people, and where did they come from?

He sped up as much as he could to put some distance between the car and their pursuers. The people also seemed to catch up to the car faster than they would have previously. That unnerved him more than he let on. As safely as he could drive on the curves, he raced away and wondered if Bridgeford would be safe after all. It wasn't as though he'd been sure before, but now, he was more than just concerned. What if there were a horde of strangers waiting for them when they arrived because they would then be aware of the car's obvious destination? Wondering if they could bypass the town somehow, he worried about where they would sleep. Could they just take turns and sleep on the road? But then, there was also a worry about Nadine taking a turn at the wheel with how much she had already been through.

Not knowing what else to do, he kept driving, looking into the trees to the sides of the road for anything dangerous.

He could see signs, real or imagined, that there had already been strangers there previously. However, when they reached the town limit, he slowed to drive around. There were no signs of habitation anywhere in the town. He had thought of trying to shelter in one of the buildings, but he wasn't sure it would be safe enough. Everything everywhere was black and empty-looking. He worried that a light in any of the windows would stand out amid all the darkness, although it looked like the power might be off everywhere anyway. The streetlamps were out, and there was no sign that anything else was operational either. He looked at Nadine and sighed.

"I don't think we should stop," he confessed.

She shook her head.

"We should try to find something to eat, then we'll go on." He remembered the deli sandwiches he had picked up the day before and asked her to hand him one. It seemed like it would be more filling than the pastry and bag of chips he had eaten earlier in the day, and he hoped it would hold him until the next day. Finding a somewhat hidden place to park, he pulled the car behind an old, darkened shopping center and away from the road.

She took the other sandwich, and they both peeled open the clear plastic wrappings. But Jackson's first bite told him the sandwich had been in the store for much longer than it should have been. The bread was extremely stale. His instinct said to throw it away, but he hated to waste anything, especially when he wasn't sure what they would find later. At his pause, Nadine looked over at him, obviously worried. He couldn't hide his expression of disgust. Finally, he just shook his head and tried to eat the sandwich. Gagging on it, he tried not to choke as he swallowed the almost tasteless meat with the musty bread. It wasn't moldy, just stale, thankfully. So, he hoped he wouldn't become ill. He managed to eat half of it, but, in the end, he couldn't finish it. He took a large swig of water to get the foul taste out of his mouth, then took another bag of chips. He saw Nadine do the same.

"That was revolting," he managed to say, suppressing the wave of nausea that threatened to come over him.

She had tears in her eyes from trying not to throw it up as she ate it, and he felt some empathy but didn't know what else they could have done. They didn't have anything else ready-to-eat. "What about one of the stores nearby? Can't we just find something to eat in one of those?" she wanted to know.

"I don't want to make any more noise and draw any more attention to us than we have already. Besides, how do we know it wouldn't be worse than what we've just eaten? What if the power is out here and everything is spoiled?" he said. She just nodded. "We'll find a place to stop. Maybe we can have some soup or something instead later on," he finished. She didn't look optimistic.

He turned the ignition back on, carefully pulled out of the driveway, then headed down the main road again, aiming for the next town. When he came to a junction, he turned toward the smaller of the two towns. However, it was the farthest away. We can't catch a break, can we? he thought.

————

CHAPTER
FOUR

Following the center stripe with the headlights, he tried to stay focused and awake. It was past two in the morning, and he was exhausted beyond words. All he could remember was driving down the dark road. Images of the concrete with trees on either side haunted him even with his eyes closed. He hadn't slept well the night before, and he was sure he would need to sleep soon, or he would fall asleep whether he meant to or not. In his fatigue, he wasn't sure anymore how far they were from the next town, and he hadn't seen a sign in a while. He was so tired that he wasn't sure he could read it with his mental fog anyway, as he couldn't even remember the town's name. It might have started with a "C," but he couldn't be sure at that point.

Nadine was trying to sleep against the window, but she couldn't relax. She kept opening her eyes at the slightest noise or bump in the road and seemed jumpy. He understood. Uncertainty was the only thing that was enough to keep him from sleeping outright. At times, he found himself blacking out for a second or two before coming to. The car hardly swerved at all. He thought he had been driving so much in the past few days that he could probably do it while sleeping.

He felt himself starting to doze off again and dared to take a hand off the wheel to wipe his eyes. The motion of the car made Nadine sit up straight.

"What happened?" she asked, nervous.

"Nothing. I just wiped my eyes. I feel like I'm falling asleep."

"Do you want me to drive?" she asked, not looking like she was anxious at the prospect.

"No. It's all right. I will manage one way or another," he replied. She looked relieved.

He wished the radio stations were operational so he could check the news, as he desperately wanted to know more about the current state of affairs. How far did it go? Was it local? Nationwide? International? The lack of information was frustrating. He felt it would help him decide what to do. But then, it must be more than nationwide because his phone wasn't working either. He could get information via satellite, but the news wasn't being updated from any of the sources he followed. When the phone died, though, he wondered how he would be able to recharge it if the power was out.

Realizing he'd started to doze off again after feeling his head drop, he looked up and tried to focus on the road again. Without food and very little sleep the night before, he was worried that he wouldn't find a safe place to rest, and then what would they do? He didn't think he could do it for much longer. He would collapse. Wiping his eyes again, he looked at the clock on the dashboard and saw that it was approaching four in the morning. He hoped the town was nearby.

When they reached the town, he could hardly believe it. He pulled off the main road and drove through the deserted streets, not expecting to see anything open anymore. He was right. Nothing was open anywhere, not just that town. But he looked for a building that looked relatively secure and older, with sturdier doors and few or no windows on the bottom floor. There weren't many of those, but there was a small-ish boutique hotel with a white brick exterior, and he parked behind the building so as not to advertise their presence. They walked around cautiously to the front door and went inside, glad the door was still unlocked. They locked it behind them, and Jackson found a small flashlight in the office behind reception in a bulky wooden desk. Then, they slowly went through the small building, room by room, with the gun and the small light, until they were certain there was no one else present. Then, they piled the heavy furniture up against the front doors and the large window on the ground level, trying to be as silent as possible. Next, they checked the back door and made sure it was still secure, as well, before pushing the desk up against the door to be sure it couldn't be opened while they were asleep. There weren't any other windows or guest rooms on that level, so he looked through the reception desk until he found an old metal key with the hotel name tag attached to it, and they went up the stairs, avoiding the elevator as they didn't think it would be operational.

Paranoid, he checked the hallways again and then went inside their room for the night. It had two beds, but Jackson wanted to block the window so they could use the light without being observed. There was some moonlight streaming in through the window, but he still wanted to try to eat something and didn't want to alert anyone that they were there. So, Nadine helped him close the blackout curtains and then pushed one of the mattresses up against the window. He tried to turn the lamp on, but it didn't work. That meant the a/c wasn't working either. The room felt like an oven. So, he ate the can of soup cold.

He barely remembered eating it. He checked his watch before the glow had gone from the hands and saw that it was after six. Then, he gestured in the darkness for her to take the bed while he tried to curl up on the chair, but it was extremely difficult. The chair wasn't very large, and although he wasn't overly tall, it was still difficult for him to fit enough of his frame into it to be comfortable. He felt her hand on his shoulder rather than saw it, and she guided him to the bed.

Then he heard her shoes squeak as she climbed into the chair. He was too tired to argue.

———

The room was still dark when he awoke, and he couldn't remember where he was or how he had gotten there. He didn't remember anything about the night before at all. Part of him wanted to keep sleeping, but he was hungry again. Stirring slightly, he realized there was something next to him. Puzzled, he reached out and felt something soft and warm lying there, and then he heard snoring. Then he was *really* confused. What *had* happened? He rubbed his eyes and tried to sit up, then slid toward the foot of the bed to get off it. In the darkened room, he carefully found the food bag again. He didn't think he could drive on just a pastry and some chips again, so he found another can of soup and started to open it, but he changed his mind, then he went into the bathroom to relieve himself and change. Instead of the dress shirt he had been wearing, he put on one of the tee shirts he usually slept in. As he didn't have any casual pants with him on that trip, he just left on the dress pants. He wanted to shower, but he decided to wait until after he'd eaten.

When he returned to the bedroom, Nadine was sitting up and looking a little mystified from what little he could determine. She gazed at him as if he could solve the mystery for her, but he just shook his head.

"I don't know what happened. I can't remember anything about last night at all," he told her.

She shook her head like she was trying to clear it, then wiped her eyes. "Nothing happened. I just couldn't sleep on the chair," she replied.

He was relieved, as he didn't want to think he was the

type of person who might have taken advantage of her in his stupor the night before. "You looked puzzled."

"Just trying to remember some things. And you look different without the dress shirt."

He almost let out a laugh. "Is that a criticism?"

She shook her head, but he could barely make out the movement.

"I know I also need some comfortable pants and shoes, just in case." He opened the can of soup, not very interested. But, after the first bite, he couldn't stop eating. When he finished the soup, he found another bag of chips and opened that, too. "We also need to replenish our food supply." He ate a few chips. "With ready-to-eat foods, of course," he added, although he was sure that much was obvious.

In the black gloom, he could just make out that she stretched her arms and stood up, going over to the bag of food and choosing another can. They still had some more canned foods, which could be eaten cold, which wasn't as unappealing in the heat, but they needed fresher foods, also. However, they were reluctant to leave that room, and they weren't sure there was anything anywhere that could be found regardless. Nadine seemed to realize she hadn't changed from the day before, and she went into the bathroom to do so and to clean her wounds with antiseptic. They had healed to some degree, but letting them get infected without the possibility of acquiring any antibiotics could be deadly.

When she came out, she was wearing the lavender dress he'd picked out with dark purple and yellow flowers on it. It brought out the brown of her eyes. Dropping his gaze, he went back to his chips. He hadn't thought about her much before and didn't want to start doing so now. She was

vulnerable and traumatized, and he didn't think it would
be fair to either of them to get into any kind of relationship,
should she be interested at all. He got up to get a bottle of
water instead.

Again, she picked up her soup, and he handed her a
bottle of water while he was up. She thanked him, then he sat
down in the chair by the desk while she sat on the floor with
her soup and ate hungrily.

"Maybe we can try to stay here today and tonight,
then leave tomorrow morning? I don't think we have enough
supplies to last any longer than that," he suggested.

She nodded.

He couldn't tell what she was thinking. Was this an
acceptable plan, or did she want to leave? Was she only
agreeing to avoid an argument, or did she really think that
was the best course of action? "We'll have to pick up some
things on the way out tomorrow, though."

She nodded again. He sipped his water. Then, he
noticed that he still had the bag of chips in his hand, and he
tried to finish them but realized he was still more tired than
he'd been aware of earlier. Setting the bag aside, he stood up
and went back to the bed. He wasn't sure if he could sleep,
but he just felt tired. At first, he debated changing into his
pajama pants, but he fell asleep before he could remove his
shoes.

———

He woke again in the same place. Slightly disoriented, he
thought he may have just dreamed about eating the soup and
chips. Upon looking around, he saw Nadine was still curled
up on the bed. So, he must have dreamed it all, then. He got
up from the bed and climbed off the end, then saw the empty

containers in the trash and realized that he did eat earlier. Then, he belatedly noticed he was wearing a tee shirt and not a dress shirt as before, and he remembered thinking he needed casual pants and shoes. So, he definitely had been up. Wiping his face with his hands, he tried to wake up some more. Then, he used the flashlight to check his watch, seeing it was almost one-thirty. However, he still hadn't slept enough to make up for the sleep deprivation from the last couple of days, and he hoped he could make it up later.

Choosing a pre-packaged pastry, he opened the wrapper, trying to be as quiet as possible so as not to wake Nadine. She stirred anyway. Cursing the cheap plastic, he decided it was best to be on a similar schedule anyway. He looked in the bag for another one and found it. "Are you hungry?" he asked her.

She shook her head. "Not yet. But thank you."

Feeling awkward, he didn't know what else to say. He nibbled on the pastry and tried not to think about going back to sleep. Watching Nadine yawn, he fought back one in response. "Is there tea or coffee?" he asked finally. Unfortunately, he wasn't sure he trusted his recollection anymore.

She got out of bed and went to stand in the dressing area. "There's a machine, but it looks like there's just coffee," she answered, feeling the counter with her hands in the blackness.

"How much does it make? Is it just one cup or—"

She felt the packet and tried to determine its dimensions. "I think just one cup. Did you want me to make it anyway?"

"Yeah. Thanks. Maybe we can share it if it's enough." The yawn he'd been fighting finally showed itself, and he wiped his face again. "Wait. Maybe save it for the morning.

I'm not sure we'll be able to get any later. I didn't think of that. Sorry."

"I haven't started it yet. It's okay." She came back into the bedroom and sat on the floor near the microwave as before. Then, she held her hand out, and he wasn't sure what it was she was asking for at first. Eventually, he handed her a pastry, and she took it and unwrapped it. But she sighed before she started to eat it.

They ate in silence for a few minutes, with Jackson trying to plan things in his head, trying to figure out how things would go and what he could do. Partly, he wanted to check out the window to see if it was safe to go out, but he was afraid to do so, afraid of what he would see. Looking at Nadine, who was staring into space again, he knew he'd tried to rescue her for a reason, and now what was he going to do? He didn't know where he could take her. For that matter, he didn't know where to go that was safe for him, either. Where *could* they go?

Initially, he thought about showering, but he decided it might be too noisy. However, he didn't know what else to do but just go back to sleep. Then again, maybe he should. They could just drive at night and sleep during the day instead. He wasn't sure which was safer, though. If they continued the way things were, would their luck hold out?

He realized he'd been staring off for a while and snapped himself out of it. Looking down at his hand, he saw that he'd finished the pastry already. He crumpled the wrapper and put it in the trash. Nadine was still absent-mindedly eating hers. Sighing, he then leaned back slightly in the chair, closing his eyes tightly and then opening them again as if that would somehow magically make everything go away. He wished it would.

When he sat forward again, he saw Nadine looking at him with a slightly worried expression. "Is everything okay?" she asked.

"No. Everything is not okay. But we'll manage, I suppose. At least, I hope so." He gave a wry smile. "Sorry. I'm not very good at being optimistic."

She slumped slightly. "No. It's hard to be right now. The way things are...."

He nodded. "Yeah."

"What should we do now?" she asked.

"I don't know. We should try to be as quiet as possible in case there are any of those...things...out there. Maybe I'll just go back to sleep. Maybe we'll just leave tonight instead of in the morning."

"If we need to stop at the store, then we should do that before it gets dark. There aren't as many of those things during the day, I don't think."

He thought a moment. "I don't know. Would you rather sleep for a couple more hours and leave now, or wait until morning and stock up then?"

Straining to see her, he watched while she debated the question. "I think we should leave tonight. I don't want to wait until they find us."

He nodded. "Okay, well, then I'm going to try to get a couple more hours of sleep. I can't drive like that again. Not yet, anyway." He stood and stretched his back, then went to bed. She got up to follow him. "You don't need to sleep if you don't want to. I just need to since I'll be driving."

She shrugged. "I'm still sleepy."

He shook his head. Whatever. Then, he lay down on the

bed and tried to push his shoes off with his feet, but Nadine reached over and took them off, then set them on the floor so as to avoid them clunking onto the floor and sounding through the building. Mumbling his thanks into the pillow, he closed his eyes. He sensed her lying down beside him, but he was too tired to see if she was awake and looking at him or if she was already trying to sleep.

―――――

Jackson opened his eyes, then allowed the room to come into focus again. Nadine was still lying beside him, not quite touching. He closed his eyes briefly before sitting up again, then wiped his face with his hands, still hoping to feel more awake and alert after sleeping so erratically. Nadine turned over and faced him, an almost smile on her face before she opened her eyes. Then, she resumed her usual melancholy expression. She must have dreamed about her boyfriend, he thought. That thought made him sad, knowing this whole situation was difficult for her, and he wished he knew what to do or say. However, he reminded himself that it really wasn't his problem. He needed to find a way to get her back to France or to another family member or friend. But what if there wasn't anyone? What if there wasn't anyone anywhere at all? He tried not to think about that possibility and climbed off the foot of the bed. Reclaiming his shoes, he then went into the bathroom. He quickly brushed his teeth and washed his face, but he didn't bother with the shower, although it was tempting with how much he'd sweated in the past couple of days.

When he emerged into the bedroom again, Nadine was sitting in the chair he'd been using during their stay, eating soup out of one of the cans. They had been reusing the plastic ware that had come with the restaurant breakfast he'd picked up the first morning. But some of the tines were broken off the forks by now. They definitely needed to restock their supplies, he thought. Looking in the bag for another can, he withdrew one at random. It was spaghetti, but he still used the other spoon instead of one of the broken forks. Sitting down on the edge of the bed, he tried to cut a meatball with the spoon then checked the time. It was after three. He guessed they needed to hurry if they wanted to be out of the town before things got bad, not knowing how long it would take at the store.

"Why don't you start the coffee now? I'll pack in a moment," he said, trying to hurry through the spaghetti. She stood and went to the small machine, filling it with water. He ate what he could reach with the flimsy spoon, then put the can aside. Quickly, he went around the room and put the few items they had removed back in their bags. He consolidated the food bag again, which was mostly empty now. Then, he emptied all the trash and went to wash his hands. Nadine was finishing her soup.

When he checked the coffee machine, he could see that there was no power to the hotel at all, as nothing had brewed. So, it hadn't just been the lights. Unfortunately, he'd been too groggy to reason it out. A little frustrated with himself for the lapse, Jackson poured the coffee grounds into the two cups provided by the hotel. Then, he poured cold water from the tap into each cup, as there didn't appear to be any hot water either, adding a small amount of powdered creamer to each one. He hated the stuff, but there wasn't anything else. Lastly, he took the two sweetener packets and let Nadine choose which one she wanted: sugar or artificial. He took the other, adding it to his cup and stirring before taking a sip and thinking he'd had much better coffee elsewhere. Maybe it was the powdered creamer. Maybe it was the fact that it had not been brewed. But, again, there wasn't much choice. He looked around the room, double-checking that they hadn't forgotten anything. Then, he hefted his overnight bag and waited for Nadine to take up hers and the food bag with the water in it. When they were somewhat ready, he carefully opened the door as quietly as possible, peering into the hallway with their tiny flashlight. It was very dark, and he couldn't make out very much. However, he could see to the stairs, which looked clear, so he silently walked toward those, checking behind them often to make sure there weren't any unpleasant surprises.

Upon reaching the ground floor, he noticed that the barricades were still in place, but he had no idea what it looked like outside. Obviously, he didn't want to advertise their presence, but he also needed to know if it was safe to leave. Looking behind them again, he tried to look out one of the windows by leaning close to the wall. It looked clear. Since he'd parked behind the building, he led them to the office and moved the desk quietly away from the back door. He peeked out of the peephole, and then he opened the door a crack to look. The car was right by the door. He didn't see anything suspicious. They went outside into heat that was only slightly less sweltering than the hot, still air inside the hotel and put their bags in the car. Then, he started the ignition.

Food was their first priority, and anything else was second. He went to another gas station, and they tried to fill the tank. While Nadine watched over the car, he went inside the empty attached convenience store and tried to take as many things as he could in a short amount of time, not seeing a clerk or any patrons anywhere around. The room was silent, without even the sound of the refrigerators to fill the void. He remembered a box of plastic ware. Then, he took more water, pastries, chips, and canned goods. He found some instant coffee, creamer, first aid supplies, and some items for hygiene. Lastly, he took a few miniature bottles of antibacterial gel. Then, he switched on the pump at the register, took the bags and ran for the car.

Again, he rethought his departure and went back inside. He took a few more items from the shelves and then went behind the counter, where he found another gun that looked like it had been in the process of being loaded, but there was blood beneath the register. He didn't look to see where the body might have gone, but he just quickly took what he could find and ran. There were only a couple of bullets, and he knew they wouldn't fit the other gun he'd found. But he took the bullets out of the gun to transport it more safely and put it in the glove compartment with the other one.

Once they were done at the gas station, clothing was harder to find. Driving around the town, they couldn't find anything that looked like it might have anything for women and men both. But then, he somehow found a military supply store as soon as he was about to give up. He couldn't believe their luck, but he was happy for the opportunity to find some proper protection from the terrors that were pursuing them. He went inside with the two guns, hoping to find more ammunition for both of them. Too nervous to take too much time to look, he put as many boxes of each one as he could into a bag, then rushed to find other clothing items for himself and Nadine. He found some cargo pants and shoes in his size, but he didn't bother trying them on. He put a camo tee in the bag and grabbed a shotgun and some shells on the way out the door. "Get some proper shoes," he told Nadine as he put the bags on the floor in the back, where he hoped they could still reach them in a hurry. "Grab them quickly. We need to leave."

She ran inside the store, and he could see her searching as she moved away from the window. He tried his best to keep watch but knew that things could change in a second, so he was extremely anxious. Eventually, when she didn't return, he started to grow worried that something had happened to her. He felt his stomach lurch at the thought. Of course, he didn't want to hit the horn unless absolutely necessary, but he contemplated it at that moment. Then, when he was about to lock up the car and go inside, he saw her run out of the store with a bag of clothes and some shoes, as well as a couple of other things he couldn't identify. She climbed hurriedly into the car without preamble.

"I was getting worr—"

"They're behind me!" she cried urgently.

He turned on the ignition, put the car in gear, and sped away, but not before seeing a glimpse of a shiny, silver frame with rotting skin hanging off it emerged from the store behind them. So, they weren't people at all. The hideous thing ran after the car as he drove, and Nadine tried not to scream as it seemed to keep up with their car and match their speed. Jackson made a turn and then pushed the gas pedal all the way down as they aimed for the main road again. Relieved, he saw the frame-like skeleton fall back in the rear-view mirror, but then suddenly, there were several more of the grotesque figures in front of the car, blocking his retreat. Quickly, he braked, then turned around, heading back the way they had come. He avoided the disgusting thing that had chased them, and he made a loop until he was heading back toward the main road, but in the wrong direction. He was heading back toward Bridgeford.

———————

CHAPTER
FIVE

"What if they *want* us back there? What if that's their intention?" Nadine asked him, upset.

"But they wouldn't necessarily have known I would go this way. What if they thought I would try to go through them? Or what if I just find another way around?" he countered.

"There isn't another way around, is there?" She sounded almost hopeful.

"I'm not sure. I don't really remember much about that day." He started to get his phone out but then remembered that he'd left it in his overnight bag. It was probably dead anyway. Even more, he regretted not picking up a map at the gas station. "No, wait. There was a junction after Bridgeford. I took the smaller road, but there was another road. We can go there instead of Bridgeford."

"But wasn't it a larger town? What if those things are there?"

He sighed. "I don't know. Maybe there's another option. We'll just have to think on it a bit." Looking over to say something else, he saw her hands shaking. Concerned, he reached out and touched them, saying, "We'll be all right." But she recoiled, and he felt like an idiot. "I'm sorry."

The apologetic look she gave him broke his heart. She shook her head as if feeling guilty for possibly upsetting him. "No. *I'm* sorry. I shouldn't—"

He pulled the car to the side of the road and parked it without turning off the engine. Turning to Nadine, he looked directly into her eyes. "Seriously, don't apologize for having boundaries. It's a good thing, not a bad thing. I wasn't thinking, all right? It's my mistake. You are not obligated to do *anything* for me. Not a thing."

A couple of tears came down, and she wiped them

away. "Okay." Her voice was a little shaky, but she nodded her understanding, and he put the car in gear and continued back onto the road.

Looking ahead, he tried to remember what the name of the other town had been and how much larger it might be. Unfortunately, he couldn't remember how far it was to the junction either. There wasn't very much time before it started to get dark again, and he didn't want to be near any of the towns when it did. He took a sip of the rancid coffee from the hotel. It wasn't any more drinkable after their two stops that afternoon, but it hadn't tasted good to start. He drank it, anyway, knowing it was more about staying alert than enjoying the taste.

Then, he remembered the items Nadine had in her bags as she ran out of the last store. "I know you picked up some shoes and some clothes, but what else did you pick up in that shop?" he asked.

She looked at him oddly. "What do you mean?"

He gestured to the bag at her feet. "You picked up some other things besides clothes and shoes. I'm just curious to know what you might have found in there."

"Oh." She picked up the bag and showed him a few stun guns. Then she took out a handful of knives. "I don't know if they will help, but we didn't have anything like them."

"The knives might be very useful, actually." He didn't want to think about close combat with any of the strangers, knowing he knew nothing about it and couldn't hold his own against any of them. But he did know that he and Nadine needed better tools. And he knew the knives would be better used as tools than weapons.

"I wish we'd had more time there. I'm sure we could have found more in there if we'd had a chance to look," she said.

"I'm sure you're right."

He was still puzzling over the town name and how far to go when Nadine asked him, "What are those things? Where did they come from?"

Realizing he'd been wondering that as soon as he'd seen them, he had been trying not to dwell on it recently. "I don't know," he answered.

"They don't seem like something we would *make*, do they? Like some sort of bio-engineering disaster? Or...I don't know. Where else would they come from?"

"I don't know," he repeated. "They're changing, though. They looked more like people before. They moved strangely, but they looked like people. Now..."

She seemed to shudder. "How long have they been here?"

He hadn't wanted to think about that at all, either. "I don't know," he said, uselessly. "What are you thinking? That they've been here all along?"

"Not necessarily. Just a long time."

"Why would you say that?"

"How else would there be so many to attack at one time, and no one would notice beforehand? Maybe they've been coming a few at a time for a long time." When she said it, it made sense, but it wasn't the only explanation, he was sure.

"But, if their intention was to attack, then why wait until we can spot them? Why not do it before we were alerted to their presence? And how did *that* happen, for that matter? How did it just happen now that we were able to spot them?

What happened to them?" Jackson countered.

She seemed to consider his words. "I don't know." She sighed. "This is a nightmare."

He agreed. "I don't know what to do other than run," he admitted.

She shook her head.

He kept driving, trying to keep to the center of the road, although there were periodic obstacles. He just didn't want to be near the trees. His speed stayed closer to the limit for safety, but part of him also wanted to go faster to keep away from whomever those people were, whatever they were. Although he now knew they weren't people, he didn't know what else to call the strange beings.

As the sun started to set, Nadine handed Jackson a sandwich. It was only marginally better than the previous one. So, he had to pull over to eat it, trying to keep it down. Making a face, he followed the sandwich with a bottle of water, then he pulled back to the road and continued toward the junction. She handed him a second bottle of water upon his request, and he kept trying to swish the stale sandwich taste out of his mouth.

Finally seeing the junction ahead, Jackson slowed the car and eventually came to a stop. He looked at Nadine. The other town was quite a bit larger than Bridgeford. It was a small city. "What do we do? I don't want to go back to Bridgeford."

She looked dismayed. "No. But we can't go the other way, either. We can't."

He thought a moment, but he didn't have any other ideas. "We'll just go through. It can't hurt to just go straight through."

She looked near tears but nodded, and he took the turn away from Bridgeford toward Capeca.

———

Jackson became more and more nervous the closer they got to the city. Naturally, he worried that the strangers would somehow know they were coming and would be waiting for them, although he didn't necessarily think that he or Nadine posed any kind of a threat. Why would two sole survivors matter to the strangers? However, he already didn't understand the strangers' motivations in any way. Why were they so set on killing everyone?

He could see Nadine's grip tighten on the seat, and then she started to wring her hands. It wasn't helping him to feel more relaxed. He tried to ignore it, but then he worried about the sound of the engine in the relative silence, and he worried about the vehicle lights in the darkness. What could he do? Slowing his speed, he hoped that would reduce some of the noise, but he didn't know what to do about the lights.

"I'm going to turn out the headlights and see if we can still see, all right?" he said. He switched them off, reducing his speed even more. The moonlight seemed bright enough to see by, but there were still the other lights on the car. So, he tried not to brake as he entered the city limits.

Again, keeping toward the center of the road, he cautiously made his way through the darkened streets, looking for another junction or turn to get them out of potential danger. He didn't want to stay there any longer than necessary. Watching as the black spectral skyscrapers emerged out of the gloom as they passed, he felt fear flood through him. Anything or anyone could be hiding in the structures, and he was terrified that they would be ambushed as they drove down the empty road. The streetlights were completely out, drawing attention to the car every time he had to slow down or stop, the brake lights gleaming red eyes in the dark. There were hardly any insect or animal sounds to mask the sound the car made, either. Everything about it seemed dangerous and overly risky. He didn't know his way around the city, but he hoped there would be a junction off the main road, and so he stayed where he was, driving through the center of downtown in a mostly darkened vehicle. There were no signs of life anywhere, but that could be misleading. It made him worry about where the attackers were. Were they waiting somewhere for any survivors to show themselves? With the rest of the population missing or possibly worse, there was no one to maintain the power grid, and everything was slowly going dark everywhere they'd been. Capeca was the first large city they'd seen in this state. Until recently, they had still been able to use the power periodically.

He saw a sign up ahead for another junction and was relieved. Slowing the car, he attempted to read the sign, trying to determine the best route and decided to turn right. Both towns seemed roughly the same size, and he didn't think it would matter greatly which one he chose. There was a chance they could be in trouble either way. He winced at the sound the tires made on the gravel as he made his way onto the other road, but he'd only gone a few feet before he saw them.

Some of them had sparks periodically flying from a joint or a facial tic, but there was no doubt they were the same people. Most of the flesh had come off the boxy metal skeletons, but they seemed to move about better without it. They didn't look like human skeletons, more angular and menacing with strange inhuman features. Illuminated by the moonlight, they shone and almost appeared to luminesce as they advanced on the car. He reversed out of position and started to go in the opposite direction, back toward the turn for the other town, but he could see more skeletons approaching from that direction, also. They were lining the road like sentries. He quickly reversed again, making a J-turn and heading back to the main road and away from the junction. There was metal hammering as the skeletons' legs pounded the pavement as they pursued the car. Ignoring the noise, Jackson sped up and rejoined the road, then gunned the engine back toward the center of the city.

He could see the glinting of metal in the taillights as he braked for a turn, feeling a crash as something collided with the side of the car. However, he didn't slow down and decided it was pointless to drive blind. He turned the headlights back on and increased his speed. There was a screeching sound from the rear, but he didn't look back. He swerved around a stalled vehicle and then pushed the gas pedal down toward the floor, hearing a sound like a piece of metal coming loose and then skittering down the road behind them.

———

Nadine's screams were dying down as they crossed out of the city limits. The skeletons lined the road behind them, blocking their passage, preventing them from returning as if to say, "This is our city now." They were definitely taking over. But to what end?

Where was safe? *Was* there any safe place? Could Jackson and Nadine stop what was happening? He had no idea what to do. For now, he just wanted a safe place to rest when the time came. So, he continued to drive. It seemed endless. He raced away from the city as fast as the now-damaged car could take them, but he had no idea how to stay safe without the car. The skeletons could outrun them on foot. What would they do if something happened to the car? He tried to keep an eye out ahead of them on the road, but he was also worried about anything that might be behind them. Frequently, he checked the rear-view mirror until he was reasonably sure they hadn't been followed.

"They're herding us toward Bridgeford," Nadine stated.

It felt that way to him, too, but he didn't want to worry her. "We'll think of something," he told her. But he had no idea what they could possibly do at that point.

It was late, and he had been hoping to stop and get some sleep the next morning. He wasn't sure when that would happen now, though. The narrow road was mostly straight and surrounded on both sides by walls of impenetrable forest. It was like driving through a tunnel, and it made him feel the pull of sleep even more. He was already exhausted from the previous bout with sleep deprivation, and the small amount of coffee he'd consumed wasn't nearly enough to compensate. At one stop, he remembered that he had picked up some instant coffee, but he didn't have a chance to get any camping gear or anything to use to heat the water. Obviously, at that point, he hadn't thought of the grid being out. Bridgeford was probably too small to have such supplies, and he still wasn't sure why the skeletons wanted them there if it were some sort of trap. He was almost sure it was. But there wasn't another direction they could go that they hadn't already tried, was there? How could they avoid the town?

He sipped his water and tried to think. The ground was too soft to attempt to go off-road, and with the car damaged, he wasn't sure he would make it anyway. Plus, there were too many trees. What else could they try? After the last attempt, he didn't think they could just go through the town unobstructed. Bridgeford had been deserted during their previous drive through it, but he doubted that was the case now. Also, where were all the people, he wondered? Where had everyone gone? He hoped it wasn't the worst-case scenario.

"I need to stop," Nadine informed him, interrupting his thoughts. He looked for a wide enough space to the side of the road and pulled over. Then, he got out of the car and checked behind some of the trees to make sure it was safe before signaling her. Thinking about it then, he decided he probably needed to do it, too.

He went back to the car to wait, and when she returned, he took his turn as quickly as he could. Running back to the car, he looked around to make sure they weren't being observed and then got into the driver's seat. He hadn't turned off the engine and just pulled back onto the road.

"I'll need fuel soon," he noted. He couldn't remember if they'd passed a gas station on the way or not. It had been dark, so they could have. The plan had been to fuel up in the city, but maybe he could do so at the junction, at least.

They drove on into the night. He had no idea what time it was, and he didn't want to check the clock, afraid it would make him feel sleepier to know for sure. So, he kept going, thinking about anything but how tired he was. Should he bother turning the headlights off at the junction? Maybe. He wasn't sure anything would be waiting for them, but he didn't want to draw attention to themselves if he could help it.

Nadine seemed introspective, also hardly saying a word. He was afraid she was thinking about her boyfriend and everything she had been through, but he didn't know how to help her through it. Of course, it really wasn't his responsibility in a lot of ways. She was no relation to him at all, and he wasn't sure she considered him to be a friend, either. He was just a person who was present in her life at that moment. But he felt partly like he was responsible as soon as he rescued her from the road. It felt like weeks ago now, but it had only been a few days.

He knew it was stupid to ask how she was doing, too. Of course, he knew the answer. She felt the same as before, helpless and scared. Obviously, he knew because he was starting to feel the same way. He didn't know how to get them out of the mess that they were in. What could he say to her anyway? Everything would seem shallow and insensitive. However, he feared that not talking about it would seem even more so.

"How are you doing?" he asked. It sounded stupid even as it came out of his mouth.

She just shook her head.

"I feel horrible about everything you've been through," he continued, wishing he could ease some of the stress she was under.

She shook her head again. "It's not your fault," she responded. Her voice cracked, but she didn't break down.

"Maybe not. I just wish I could help you."

"You did help me. No one else did." She let out a breath and looked toward him. "It's okay. Really. I think we'll be lucky just to get through this. I'm worried about what's going to happen in Bridgeford. I don't want to...I just hope we'll be okay. I can deal with everything when this is over." She turned back to the road.

"Okay." He knew that wasn't all of it, but he could tell she was done talking about it. "I'm sorry, though."

He kept driving, staying to the center line. Every now and then, he would slow to pass a stalled vehicle or some debris in the road, which he tried not to think about. It was never just "debris." And the stalled vehicles weren't just the vehicles, although he did his best to avoid looking inside as he passed. He kept his eyes ahead and tried to look for anything hidden to the sides of the road. The moonlight cast black shadows in the trees, making that difficult. He watched the road signs and tried to estimate the miles he'd driven so he could come up on the junction without the lights.

As they approached, he turned the lights out, hoping there would be a gas station nearby. However, there was nothing but the junction, and he paused the car in front of the sign so that he could think, seeing that there were no other options but to head back where they had already been or to go on toward Bridgeford. The car sat near-silently on the road while he tried to figure out an alternative.

"What are we going to do?" he asked no one in particular, feeling frustrated and trapped.

Nadine looked slightly scared that he didn't already have a plan. "I don't know," she answered.

He didn't want to do what the skeleton things were forcing them to do. But he didn't see any other options. He thought about returning to one of the other towns again and doing what they might not expect, but he wasn't sure it would make a difference. Would the skeletons still be there waiting? He assumed they would be. They would find a way to force the car where they wanted it to go. But why would they care? Why did it matter to trap this one car? Or were there other survivors they were trying to herd, too?

And the things really looked nothing like skeletons. How could they have gotten here? Where did they come from? There was something about them that seemed almost familiar, but he couldn't place it in his mind. He thought they would have been noticed by now if they had been there a long time, but then they had definitely looked human before. What could have happened to them? Was there a way to stop them? For some reason, he remembered the way they had converged on Smithton Lake. Was there significance to that at all? Or had there been millions of them converging on other large cities all at once?

Then, remembering Smithton Lake, he thought of the strange objects he had photographed there. He had wondered about them at the time because he had never seen things like them before, but now, he thought they looked similar to the skeleton things they had been fleeing. The objects resembled parts of the skeletons, some old and some new. Could the skeletons have been there that long? The lab had obtained parts of them, or devices made from similar technology, and needed, what…evidence? A record? He wasn't sure it mattered anymore, but had the lab realized the significance of what they'd found? Was there a way to use those objects against the skeletons somehow? Could they determine a weakness of some sort? He wanted to go back to the lab, back to Smithton Lake. Maybe all he needed were the images. Would his view camera still be there in the parking lot where he'd left it?

He realized he'd been sitting still, thinking, for several minutes. Eventually, he looked over at Nadine, who looked frightened and confused. "I'm sorry. I'm just thinking about what to do. I think I saw something in Smithton Lake, something that might help us, but I would understand if you didn't want to go back there. I'm not sure we could get there safely. I don't want to go back the way we got out but in a loop around. Still, I don't know if it will help or not."

"I don't want to go back there."

"I don't know what else to do. I don't want to go to Bridgeford. I don't want to just keep running, either. But I also know there were probably thousands of those skeleton things in Smithton Lake. It would be so dangerous that I'm not sure it would be worth the risk. But I feel like it might be the only way to determine if they have a weakness. I think I have images of them on my camera. They're high-definition, and we might be able to...." Then, he remembered the grid being out. How could they view the images large enough to analyze them? Sighing, "Actually, we may have to get into the lab where I was shooting."

"But we barely made it out of there!"

He thought a moment. "The lab is on the outskirts of the town. The skeleton things were converging on the city itself. We might have a little time before we're found. We could still take the objects with us and run."

"I don't like the 'before we're found' part of that statement."

He sighed again. "I know. I don't want to do it, either. But I don't want to keep doing this forever. We'll get caught either way. I don't want to force you to come with me, but I don't know where to take you."

Tears welled up in her eyes, and she was visibly shaking. "Please don't make me go there."

"I can take you anywhere. Just let me know where."

She shook her head. "I'm not sure anywhere is safe. I don't know."

Jackson knew she was traumatized beyond what he could imagine. He didn't want to force her to relive it as he didn't want to go back either. But he hoped it would help to end the nightmare altogether. "I still think I need to go there. We need something to work with. I think we can analyze what's in the lab where I last photographed and figure out how to disable them or how to fight them or...something."

She was obviously thinking, but he knew she didn't like what he was saying. It was likely she was trying to decide how important it was to stay with him, but she was also probably feeling like she had no other choice.

"I don't know what else to try," he added.

She looked over at that and nodded, resigned. "Okay. We'll go, but if we can't get to the lab, we'll leave, okay?"

"Definitely. I don't want to chance getting caught, either. So, we have to go back then. I can't go to Bridgeford if we're going to loop around the other way. That means we have to turn right and go back to that other town where we last stopped."

She nodded again.

———

He passed a gas station on the way to the town and had to turn around to go back. Driving up to the pump, he turned off the ignition and hurried into the attached kiosk, looking around as carefully as he could in the dark for a release. Then, he rushed back out to the car to fuel the tank. A larger flashlight and batteries would have been nice, and he remembered the store where they had found their military gear. Perhaps they should pick up more supplies if it were safe enough, he thought.

Once the tank was full, he quickly replaced the nozzle and started the car. Then, he drove on toward the town. He knew they would probably arrive in the morning, and he hoped the skeletons would be somewhere else so that he and Nadine could get some sleep and leave the next evening, as before. If not, he had no idea what to do. The car definitely wasn't safe enough to sleep in on its own.

He had been ignoring it, but he had blisters on his feet from driving in his dress shoes the past few days. Also, he wanted to change into the casual pants he'd picked up. The main reason was that he wanted to have more freedom of movement in case they had to run, which seemed likely, considering everything that had happened to them so far.

"I'm going to pull over for a bit. Sorry." He pulled the car over to the side of the road, not sure if they would be able to stop in the town or not, but knowing he needed to change regardless. Turning off the engine to save gas, he then climbed into the back seat. "I'm not going to try anything. I just need to change out of these clothes. I don't know if I'll get to do it in the town, and if we need to do any running, I'd rather be properly dressed."

He looked for the bag of clothes and shoes he'd brought from the supply store and found the pants and shoes. As he took off his old shoes, he let out a sigh of relief. "You can... er...keep your eyes to the front, all right?" He struggled out of the old pants and into the new ones, then decided to change into the camo tee he'd found, also. Briefly, he looked up to make sure Nadine was okay, but he caught her glancing in his direction. Putting on the tee, he looked out through the rear window behind the car. "Is everything all right?" he asked, putting on the new shoes.

She nodded. "Just making sure."

"I said I wouldn't try anything."

She shrugged. He tried not to sigh, but he climbed back into the front. "You're welcome to change now while it's still dark and I can't see you, or you can wait until we reach the town. It's up to you."

Shrugging again, she climbed into the back, taking her bag with her. He tried to keep his gaze out the windows and on the mirrors to make sure nothing was approaching the car and that they were safe. But he could tell she was dressing from the movements in the back of the car, and he purposely looked everywhere but there. When she climbed back to the front, she was wearing a green tank top with cargo pants and some running shoes. "Is that it? Do you need anything else?"

She shook her head. "No, I'm done."

He nodded, then started the car up again. "Hopefully, we can stop at the same hotel as last time. If not, I don't know."

Pulling the car back onto the road, he resumed their course toward the town. She handed him a small bag of chips so he could eat something, as the canned goods were too hard to eat while driving. However, after the bag of chips, he almost felt hungrier than before. "Is there any chance I could have something more filling?" Jackson asked Nadine.

She looked apologetic. "There really isn't anything."

"A pastry. Beef jerky. Whatever we've got."

She looked in the bags and found a stick of jerky, which she opened and handed to him. He took it reluctantly as he didn't want to eat anything too salty after the chips, but he didn't have many options. With the chewy texture, however, it was difficult for him to drive and eat without jolting the car. Finally, she took it from him and started to tear bites off with her fingers, which she would hand to him as she went along. When the jerky was gone, he downed an entire bottle of water and asked for another, which he set into the cup holder for later.

"Thank you," he said.

Eventually, the sun began to rise, and he knew they were approaching their destination. Anxiety filled him. He had no idea if there were any dangers awaiting them, but he had no choice but to keep driving. The best thing would be to get a few hours of sleep, at least, before they would have to leave. Obviously, he wasn't sure if driving to Smithton Lake was the best idea, but he knew they couldn't drive toward a known trap. He wasn't even sure there was any real alternative to going back to the start anyway. But what else could possibly help them to stop the skeletons? Where else was he sure to find the technology that they needed?

Then, he thought about their small arsenal of weapons and realized they would probably need a lot more than they had if they were going to eventually end up at Smithton Lake. Also, he thought he might want weapons practice before being in a more intense life-threatening situation. Hopefully, they would have a chance.

Approaching the town, they drove through on the main road and headed back toward the hotel where they'd stopped before. He didn't see any signs of the skeletons, but that didn't mean they weren't there. The sun was higher in the sky as they parked behind the building as before, and he carefully opened the rear door to the hotel and went inside. It was dark, so he took the flashlight out of his bag he had found during their first trip and tried to see if there was anything amiss.

They walked through the building with Jackson carrying his handgun ready, seeing their barricades from the previous stay still in place. But he checked to make sure the doors were still locked, as well. When they reached the upstairs rooms, they checked each one before going back to barricade the back door for safety. Then, they picked the same stifling room they'd slept in previously and went inside. Jackson pushed the table and chairs up against the door before lying, exhausted, on the bed. Then, he remembered his shoes and sat up to remove them before lying down again. He didn't wait to see what Nadine was going to do. He didn't care. All he wanted to do was sleep. Setting the flashlight down next to him, he closed his eyes.

———————

CHAPTER

SIX

When Jackson opened his eyes, all he could see was blackness. He looked toward the windows, afraid it was nighttime, but there was no way to tell. The curtains and furniture they'd used to cover the windows blocked most of the light anyway. Picking up the flashlight next to him, he accidentally brushed Nadine's sleeping form on the bed. He sat up and tried to get out of bed without waking her. However, she stirred as soon as he'd moved. In his fatigue, after checking his watch, he was confused as to whether it was one in the afternoon or one the next morning. He wiped his face to wake up, then climbed off the foot of the bed and shuffled sleepily to one of the windows, using the flashlight to keep from stubbing his toe. Then, he carefully leaned against the wall to try to see around the curtain without moving it. Seeing the sun still in the sky, he was relieved.

He still didn't think he'd had enough time to sleep, and he debated staying the night. Partly, he was afraid the car would be spotted, although it was not the only car in the lot. But he knew what had happened to some of the other people, having seen the evidence, and he wasn't sure if the skeletons could figure out that someone new was in the building. He'd put one of the guns back in his overnight bag for safety, but he didn't bring all the weapons they had. Nadine might have brought a stun gun and some knives, but he hadn't seen if she'd put the other handgun in her bag. He hoped that what they had was enough.

As he moved back toward the table, he took out the food bag and found a can of soup. Desperately, he wanted freshly cooked food, but he knew it might be a long time before either of them could have any. Opening the box of plastic utensils he'd obtained, he took out a spoon. Then, he sat in one of the chairs and unenthusiastically started eating.

Nadine took some time getting out of bed, and he knew then that he would probably have to stay until at least the next day. He didn't want to leave at night and knew that even late afternoon was fairly dangerous. But he couldn't think straight, and he knew she wouldn't try to sleep in the car, no matter how sleep-deprived she might be.

He reached into the bag and found another can, then took out another spoon. Then, he took the items to Nadine, who was sitting on the edge of the mattress, trying to clear her head. She took the soup and spoon, then sleepily opened the can and took a small bite. He returned to his seat at the table and finished his own meal, but he couldn't decide if he should try to get more sleep or wait until later in the day. Instead, he went to take care of personal hygiene in the bathroom. However, after brushing his teeth and washing his face, he didn't think he could leave it at that, although he remembered that there was no hot water. But he undressed and got into the shower with the soap and shampoo previously provided by the hotel, hoping that the noise he'd been afraid of before wasn't an issue after all.

Trying to keep it short, he hurried through the routine, then turned the water off and took a towel to dry himself. He quickly dressed back in the tee and cargo pants, then returned to the bedroom. Nadine was still sitting on the edge of the bed, eating. He took out one of the few remaining bottles of water and opened it, sitting in the chair he'd vacated earlier. She barely looked up.

"I'm not sure we should leave just yet. I'm too tired to drive, I'm afraid." He wiped his eyes again as if to demonstrate.

She just nodded in return, looking too tired to speak.

"I don't want to leave at night, so it will probably be tomorrow morning. I hope that isn't a mistake. I don't want to do anything that isn't safe, but I don't see how I could possibly make it until we reach the next town before I sleep again."

She nodded again.

He waited for more, but there was nothing else. Taking a few sips of the water, he then went back to the bed and crawled into it, trying to avoid making Nadine move. After he turned out the small light, he tried to go back to sleep.

However, he heard a sound like she had finished her soup and set it on the nightstand. Then, she took the light from him and went into the bathroom. Finally, he heard the water turn on, and he knew she was taking advantage of the chance to shower, also. He tried to ignore her and go to sleep, but he couldn't relax. Several minutes later, he heard the water turn off, and he hoped she would settle down long enough for him to sleep. Hearing her dress in the bathroom, he then heard the door open. When he opened his eyes briefly, he saw the small beam of light as she carefully walked back to the bed. She turned it off and set it beside him again before climbing back under the covers.

Again, he tried to sleep, closing his eyes. A few seconds passed, then he felt, more than heard, Nadine crying. He guessed he should have expected it sooner, but he didn't know what he could say. He knew what was bothering her, but he couldn't bring back her boyfriend, nor could he take away any of the horrors of seeing him brutally murdered. It wasn't as though he were trying to be a replacement for anyone, either. What could he say or do at this point? Would it help her to talk about it? Would it be better for her to deal with it on her own? He thought it wouldn't. But he didn't feel

qualified to be her therapist and wasn't sure exactly how to
start the conversation.

"I'm sorry, Nadine," he said.

He heard a sniffle, and then she started sobbing.
Hopefully, he hadn't made her feel worse than before.

"I didn't mean to upset you...." he started.

She shook her head in the darkness, still crying. "It's
not about you," she cried.

"No, of course, it isn't. I just meant...." He paused,
thinking he wasn't helping very much. "I don't want you to
think I don't care. If you need to say something, you can say
something."

"What can I say? I miss David. I wish none of this
had happened. I wish I hadn't fought with him that night. I
wish...." She sighed, sniffling again. "I just can't believe this
happened. I keep hoping it's just a bad dream, and I'll wake
up."

"Yeah. I definitely can understand that part." He felt
her turn to face him, although he could barely see her.

"I'm sorry, too. It's not that I don't appreciate what
you've done. I don't mean to close up, but you're a reminder
that this happened at all. As long as you're here, it means
David isn't. It's not your fault. I'm not blaming you, but I
can't help but feel that I wish David was here with me."

"I don't expect you not to miss him. I don't expect
anything. I just want to help." He felt slightly exasperated,
wishing he could be enough to comfort her. But what would
that mean exactly? Would they end up together forever or
just for the next few days? What did he want anyway? It was
a crazy time to have to make a lifetime decision. Nothing in
the past few days made any sense at all anyway. If he didn't

have his own life sorted out, how could Nadine?

"But...." She took a deep breath. "I do appreciate that you helped me. I do appreciate that you're still helping me. You didn't have to and still don't have to, but you do anyway. I hope you don't think that I resent you or anything. If I talk about it, it seems more real. I don't want that to happen."

He thought a moment, not sure how to reply. "I don't want it to be real, either. Trust me. But I do think we both need to open up sometimes. Me, included. Each of us may be the last person the other sees for a very long time. I don't know what happened or if there are any other survivors, but it might be a while before we find them. If we don't, then we will both need to help each other. So, I hope you understand that it's not just about either one of us. We'll both have to talk about this, even if it isn't right now. And you don't have to stay with me, either. If we find others, I'd understand if you want to leave."

He could hear her breathing, then she touched his face, startling him. But she seemed to be trying to gauge his expression in the darkness and how he was feeling more than anything else. "Then, where would you go?" she asked plaintively.

He shook his head. "I guess it would depend on what happens. Maybe we'll find a whole group of people in the next town, and you'll be safe. Maybe we can end this in Smithton Lake. Maybe it will be a few days or maybe a year away, but we don't know what will happen to either of us. But you don't have to stay if you don't want to. I understand for now because there's no one else. But later...."

Her hand paused, and she took it away. "I don't know if I want to think about later. It might be worse than right now," she complained.

"But it might not be. We have to hope it will be better, or otherwise, what are we here for?"

"I don't know," she answered in a small voice.

"I just mean we should keep trying. Don't give up, okay?"

He felt her nodding, but she sounded like she was still crying as she said, "Okay."

"Are you all right?" he asked, unable to judge her expression.

"Yeah. I'll be fine," she replied. "Thank you." He thought he could tell she was wiping her eyes, but he couldn't be sure.

"It's not a problem." Part of him felt like he should say more, but he didn't know what else to add. "You can always talk to me, Nadine. If you need to ask something or get something out, you can do that. You don't have to wait for me to ask. I'm not going to leave you unless you want me to."

"I didn't want to upset you because I didn't want you to take it personally. It's not about what you've done or what you didn't do. It's just everything that's happened. And I don't want you to leave me. I don't want you to think I don't want you here."

"Okay. Then, let's just agree to talk to each other. We need to be able to cooperate and work together somehow. I know I can open up, too, so it's not about you only. But sometimes, I feel like it's difficult to tell what you're thinking or feeling, and I don't want to invade your privacy by asking. You don't have to tell me, but if I'm asking a question and don't get an answer, that's putting all the pressure on me." He hoped he didn't sound too pushy or like he was angry with her.

"I'll try to talk more."

"It wasn't necessarily a criticism. I know you've been through a lot. But we've both lost everything, and now I have no one to talk to but you. I would hope you'd be understanding enough to at least respond to me. If it's a simple yes or no, it's fine, but—"

"I'm sorry. I didn't think about that. I will try. I promise." She sounded slightly regretful.

"Thank you," he said. "I don't want to worry you, but I am actually scared to go to Smithton Lake. I've been scared since this started. I'm trying to act like I know what to do, but I've obviously never been in this situation. I don't want to have anything happen to you that's ultimately my fault."

"At least you tried, but no, I don't want that either."

He couldn't tell if it was an attempt at a joke, but he gave a short laugh anyway. "Okay, so we'll work together to make sure that doesn't happen."

She sighed, then he could feel she was wiping her eyes again. "Yeah."

"Did I say something?"

"No. I just think I'm sleepy, and maybe I'll feel better later." He heard her yawn lightly, then she shifted position, and he could tell she was drifting off. He closed his eyes again.

Jackson woke a few hours later, unsure of the hour and still feeling groggy, but he was hungry again. He wanted to check his watch, but he didn't want to wake Nadine. Carefully, he tried to sit up, but he could hear her stir slightly as soon as he'd moved. Feeling around for the small flashlight, he picked it up and moved toward the foot of the bed so Nadine wouldn't have to get up. However, as soon as he was off the bed, he heard her yawning.

"What's wrong?" she said.

"Nothing. I'm just hungry," he answered. He used the flashlight to search the food bag. At that point, he knew they would need supplies before leaving the town, and he hoped they would still be undiscovered the next day.

He found another can of something, he wasn't quite sure, unable to read the label even with the flashlight. But he took a fork from the new box of utensils and opened the lid. It still wasn't easily identifiable, even after tasting it. It was vaguely tomato-y, but that was all he could say. Putting the light down, he ate it anyway. Nadine was trying to walk toward the light without stubbing her toe, and he handed her something from the bag when she reached him. Then, he made the room slightly dimmer by turning the light downward and setting it down on the table. There was still a small amount of illumination, but he hoped it wouldn't show through the windows.

"What time is it?" Nadine asked.

Picking the light up briefly to check, he set it down again. "Six." He heard her open the can and then the clink as the fork touched the sides as she ate.

"We're not leaving now, are we?"

"No. Not yet," he said, as quietly as possible. "I still think we should wait."

She was sitting on the edge of the bed, eating. "I think so, too." She mimicked his tone by almost whispering.

He finished his can of whatever it was and picked out a pastry. Then, he unwrapped that and ate it, too. Still feeling hungry, he also felt conflicted as he didn't want to eat the last of their food.

Nadine set her empty can on the nightstand, then lay back on the bed. "May I have some water?"

Taking two bottles, he walked back to the bed and handed her one before climbing in beside her, still taking care not to touch her. After her reaction before, he didn't want to make her nervous or make her think he wanted anything. He drank a little from his water bottle, then set it on the other nightstand and turned the little light off. Although he was bored, he wanted to sleep as much as possible so they would be as quiet as possible. But he could feel her moving as she drank some water, and then she got up to use the bathroom. He tried not to groan in frustration. He was tired, but he knew she might not be.

When Nadine returned, very carefully crossing the room in the black gloom, he felt the mattress dip when she sat down and then felt the covers move slightly as she lay down. She was still for a few moments, and he tried to go back to sleep. Managing to sleep for a couple of hours, he then felt something wake him, and at first, he wasn't sure what it could have been. Eventually, he noticed he could feel her trembling. Not understanding what was wrong, he was afraid he had offended her somehow. Then, he heard it. She wasn't trembling because of him at all. There was a metallic pounding sound outside the hotel, out in the street. Sounds like hundreds of the skeletons coming closer (the clanging noises as their legs hit the concrete) were resonating through the walls.

Nadine's shivering grew more intense as they heard one of the skeletons approach below their window, and despite his reservations, he leaned close and put a hand over her mouth to keep her quiet, and he held her. Her tears streamed down to his fingers, but he whispered to her that it would be all right and hoped the thing was unaware that anyone was above it. He wanted to remain as still as possible. Nadine was breathing heavily, but he could tell she was forcing herself to try to stay calm. Eventually, they heard the skeleton moving away slowly. But there were still more outside, and he felt a chill despite the suffocating heat of the room.

There were still many more skeletons walking around. The clanging was loud, but he didn't know how well they could hear or if they used sound in that way at all. If one of them was right under the window and it wasn't walking, it might be able to hear something, but he hoped none of them could. Nadine's breathing became ragged as a group of them seemed to come right up to the window, and he could feel his own voice becoming desperate as he whispered, "We're going to be fine," over and over. He hoped it was true. He repeated it like a prayer, hoping that if he said it enough that it would happen. But when the things paused, he was silent, not saying a word. His hand started to shake a little, and he was sweating from the heat and from fear, but he kept still. Then, the things moved away again. He barely relaxed.

Neither Nadine nor he could sleep with the cacophony of sounds outside the hotel. It went on for what they knew was several hours. His arm started to go to sleep, but he was afraid to move. Were they all over the town or just near the hotel? It was hard to tell. It sounded like the skeletons must be scattered around the entire town. He could hear them in the distance, too, if he could only steady his breathing long enough. There was no way to slip past unseen. The two of them were trapped, and he was too afraid to even get up to get the gun out of his bag. They both lay frozen in position, barely moving until they could hear the things going away to wherever it was that they went during the day. Jackson and Nadine were both exhausted, and Nadine started to cry in relief. Turning, she put an arm around him and wept into his shoulder. "We're going to be fine," he told her again, letting out his breath and hearing his voice crack slightly. He squeezed his eyes closed, not quite believing that they were still alive.

He opened his eyes again. There was light snoring next to his ear, and the events of the previous night came back to him. Nearly panicking, he didn't know how long he had been asleep. Abruptly, he pulled his arm out from under Nadine's head and then searched for the flashlight. When he found it, he checked his watch and sighed. It was only about nine. Maybe they would leave around ten and stock up on their supplies again. He wanted to get some better weapons. If there were that many of the skeletons here, it would be worse in Smithton Lake, and he knew for certain that what he and Nadine had now wasn't adequate.

She sat up at his sudden movement, and he quickly said, "I just didn't know how long I'd been asleep. Sorry."

"Is it late?" she asked.

"No, not too late. We should probably eat something because we don't know when we'll get to eat again. Then, we'll get more supplies and get out of here."

She nodded and yawned, stretching. He climbed out of bed, using caution to try to avoid any obstacles, and he picked out two pastries and some chips for himself and for Nadine. Taking them back to the bed, he sat down, handed some of the food to her and then felt a strong urge to go back to sleep. However, he opened the pastry instead and ate it.

He could hear her eating her pastry as well while he worried about leaving the hotel. It had been relatively safe until the previous night. What would happen when they left? Was there a trap laid somewhere? Instead of letting his thoughts get carried away, he got up and went to the bathroom to take care of his regular morning routine. When he returned, he felt slightly better, although he would have preferred another shower with how hot the room had been during their stay. He picked up some water on his way back to the bed and handed one to Nadine.

"Thank you," she said.

"No problem," he answered back.

She put a hand on his arm. "No. I mean, for last night. Thank you."

He was confused. "What do you mean?"

She seemed to be unsure of how to say what she was thinking. "You tried to keep me from being scared. I appreciate it. I probably would have given us away without meaning to."

"Oh. Well, it's all right. I didn't want to be discovered either." He grinned, and then realized she probably couldn't see it. "Either way, you were terrified, and I didn't want you to be."

"Thank you."

"Okay. You're welcome." He stood, then returned to his bag to pack up his few possessions. He didn't want to become attached to her, and he didn't want her to become attached to him, either. She might have to leave, and if he found a safe place for her to stay so that she wouldn't be going into Smithton Lake with him, he would leave her there. Hopefully, they would find other survivors, and everything would be okay, and they could stop the skeletons somehow and rebuild everything. But he was well aware that everyone he cared about might already be dead. He might truly be alone. Sighing without meaning to, he tried not to dwell on it. However, part of him was scared that if he left Nadine with other survivors, he might never see anyone else ever again. The thought was more terrifying than he wanted to admit.

Nadine went into the bathroom before packing, taking the light with her. Then, she handed it back to him when she returned while she tried to see in the dim space ahead of her. They gathered their things as quickly as possible, thinking they would still have to get food before they could go back to the military supply store to get more weapons, despite the fact that they hadn't used the ones they already had. Jackson only knew it was just a matter of time, and he knew they probably wouldn't have as good an opportunity to arm themselves again as they would there.

When they were reasonably sure they had everything packed, he took the light, and they moved the table and chairs back from the door. He feared opening it and seeing what might be outside, but he felt they had no choice. They couldn't stay another night, knowing the skeletons might return. Checking the peephole first, he then opened the door slowly and quietly. He saw nothing but the carpet and the yawning black hallway. Finally, he cautiously shone the light down toward the stairs, and it appeared to be clear. Nadine followed him back downstairs, where they checked to be sure the office still seemed secure, hoping that if it had not been breached, then they were still safe. Jackson checked through the peephole on the back door after quietly pushing the desk away from it and didn't see anything out by their car. Looking back at Nadine, who nodded, he then opened the door a crack and peeked out. Fortunately, he saw no evidence that the skeletons that were present the night before were still out and about. He hurried Nadine to the car, and they quickly dumped their belongings into the back seat and drove away.

Stopping at the previous trip's grocery store, Jackson hurriedly went through the building, focusing on water and foods that didn't need to be cooked, as well as restocking their first aid supplies, just in case. Then, he took some batteries and a larger flashlight, just in case. He took as much as he could carry quickly and rushed out of the store, not wanting to be caught off-guard.

When they got to the military supply store, however, he was much more nervous. They had almost been caught there before. Of course, he didn't know a lot about weapons, so he just tried to clean out the store and grab as much as he could especially larger-capacity weapons. Bagging items as he went, he grabbed extra magazines and as much ammunition as he could carry, still not sure it was enough. He made several trips to drop bags into the car, as well. Unfortunately, he didn't think he could stay as long as he probably needed to in order to figure everything out. When he thought he heard a noise behind the store, he ran to the door and saw Nadine looking worried in the passenger seat. Opening the driver's side door, he practically threw the last bags of ammunition and guns toward the back as he jumped into the seat and started the ignition. He reversed away from the store as quickly as possible and raced away, not bothering to look back.

On the main road, he thought he could hear the metallic

sounds of some of the skeletons behind them, but he sped on, heading out of the town and out toward the countryside. He hoped they might be able to make at least one more stop before reaching Smithton Lake, and he hoped it would be safe. But they probably couldn't stay the night in the city. Perhaps he could find more survivors, and they would have help. However, he also knew that sometimes survival forced people to do things they would never do normally. What if the others they found chose to shut Jackson and Nadine out instead of helping them?

———

When he felt they were far enough from the previous town, he pulled the car over to go through their arsenal. Nadine and he both tried to load the weapons and figure out how to use them, hoping they could figure out how to reload quickly in an emergency. Matching the bullets they'd bought to each weapon and magazine, they loaded the extra magazines and then emptied them so that they could do so again, over and over. Practicing the loading of the weapons took a while, but then they loaded as many of the magazines as they could and scratched the needed weapon and ammo into the surface with Nadine's knives so that they could refer to it later in a hurry if need be. They fired test shots and tried to hit targets they carved on some trees. At first, their shots were nowhere near the marks, but they improved slightly after trying to brace their feet firmly while keeping their knees slightly bent. Jackson didn't think he and Nadine were very good shots, but given the number of skeletons, he figured they didn't need to be terribly accurate but just as destructive as possible. Then, they made sure the extra magazines were full again, as well. When he thought they were as prepared as they could be in such a short time, he loaded everything back into the car and drove back onto the road. He hoped they would never need to use the guns, but he knew that they would definitely need a way to defend themselves, either from the skeletons or from other survivors wanting to steal their supplies. His first hope was for cooperation, and he wasn't even sure there were any others, but he wanted to be realistic.

As the car drove closer to the next town, he couldn't help but be somewhat introspective, which was just what he had wanted to avoid. He wanted to be able to speak to Nadine about anything that was bothering him, but he also didn't want to worry her unnecessarily. However, he remembered telling her that they both needed to open up to each other. He might never see another person ever again. What would he do if he had no one he could talk to? What about Nadine? If he didn't confide in her, would she feel comfortable talking to him? He knew he needed to find a way to start a conversation, but he felt he had never been that type. Even now, he felt awkward with her for some reason, even after all they'd been through together, and he knew most of it was a fault within himself. He didn't want to be emotionally committed in any way. But he couldn't afford to do that here, could he? But what if they were committed, and then something happened to either one of them? Could either one of them bear the loss after everything that had happened already? Then, he realized he was already somewhat committed, whether he liked it or not. He felt protective of her and worried about her. He didn't want to think about whether he liked her as a person or not, but maybe he needed to put aside any doubts. Obviously, he didn't have a choice, did he? What if there weren't any other people anywhere?

"You're very quiet," Nadine observed. "Is everything okay?"

He snapped out of his trance and said, "Yeah. Yeah. Everything is fine." Then, his thoughts of opening up came back to him, and he thought he had to voice at least some of his concerns. It would do him no good to keep everything to himself. He needed a sounding board as much as she did. "I'm just trying to over-plan things," he joked lightly. Then, more seriously, "I keep worrying about how things are going to go when we get there."

"Like what?" she asked.

He resisted the urge to sigh. Why become frustrated with her? It wasn't her fault that he wasn't naturally social. "I suppose I'm worried about what will happen if something should happen to either one of us. I hope I'm not making a mistake by going back there. I just don't want to keep driving forever. I don't think we'll survive long that way, either. I'm just confused as to what to do. Do you think this is the right decision?"

She thought a moment. "I don't know either, but I agree that we can't just keep driving forever. It's getting harder and harder to avoid those things."

"Do you think there might be others out there? People who have escaped and are hiding?"

"Possibly. We can't be the only ones," she replied, not sounding very sure.

"Do you think it would be worth it to try to reach some of them? What if they're just as hostile to us as those skeleton things?"

She shook her head. "They won't be the same. There must be some people out there who would want our help."

"What if we're the ones needing help?"

She paused. "I don't know."

He tried to keep his eyes on the road. "I'm worried I won't find a way to stop those skeletons or whatever they are. And I don't know what made them attack, to begin with, or what happened to them. They passed as people once, I'd assume."

"Probably."

"So, what do you think they are? Where did they come from? I just want to use whatever we find in Smithton Lake to stop them. I wish I'd known, when I was there, that something was going to happen so that I could have stolen some of the artifacts I photographed."

"You couldn't have known. And if you had tried, you wouldn't have been there to help me." She seemed somewhat embarrassed that he had to rescue her at all.

"Do you think we'll find what we need in Smithton Lake? Should we be doing something else?" he asked.

"I don't know. I don't know what was there."

He thought a while. Was it worth the trouble to go back? Should he find another solution? "I just saw things that didn't seem important at the time. They didn't make sense until I saw the skeletons. The skeletons and the artifacts look similar, like the artifacts were just parts of the skeletons that had been found. Either that or they're related somehow, the same technology."

"Are you *sure*?" She seemed to be looking for a way out.

He sighed. "No, I'm not sure. But where else can we go to get more information about those skeletons?" She looked hurt and like he'd reprimanded her. Just what he'd been trying to avoid, he'd upset her by voicing his concerns. "I'm not upset at you. I'm just concerned. I don't want to put us in harm's way for nothing. If you can think of anything else... anything...then please, tell me. I don't want to do the wrong thing."

Her eyes teared up. "No. I can't think of anything else. I don't want to go there, though."

Wanting to comfort her, he knew he really couldn't. There was nothing he could say that would change anything. He just wanted to try to make a life again. "I don't either. But maybe we can get clues there. We don't have to go all the way into the city, though. The lab is on the outskirts of town. Maybe it won't be as dangerous as going into the city proper." He tried to sound hopeful.

"My boyfriend's house wasn't in the city proper, either. I still don't think it will make a difference," she reminded him frantically.

Almost snapping at her, he tried to control himself. He didn't want to lose his temper just because she was scared. "Then, please tell me you have an idea how to end this. Please, tell me you have an idea how to stop them so we can stop running."

"I don't." She looked disheartened. "I wish I did. I wish I'd thought of something days ago."

Right then, he wanted to pull the car over again so they could have a proper conversation. But instead, he felt like he had to keep heading toward the city. They had a long way to go still. "I know," he told her. "Me, too."

A few tears escaped her eyes before she wiped them away and composed herself. "Okay. So, we'll go. But we'll have to plan how to get in and out quickly."

"I might be able to drive up to the building where the artifacts were stored. There was a large parking lot, but there weren't stairs leading to the buildings, and the concourse was fairly wide in between them. I think I could potentially fit the car through and up to the building or close anyway. The hard part will be getting into the lab and all without searching methodically through every room to be sure there aren't other occupants."

"We'll be armed," she said.

———————

CHAPTER
SEVEN

They entered another deserted town, with more empty streets and abandoned buildings. At least there were a few hours of daylight left, Jackson thought. He drove the car down the main road, looking for a shop with food and supplies. There wasn't much to choose from, and he felt frustrated and tired. Just so tired. Part of him was definitely apprehensive about going into Smithton Lake. Who was he to think he had the power to stop the skeletons?

Then, he switched off that part of his mind and tried to focus on food and water and medical supplies. He turned a corner and saw a medium-sized drugstore. It would have to do. As quietly as he could, he turned into the store's parking lot and turned off the engine. "Let's restock our supplies here," he suggested. Although, even after their conversations about opening up, he still felt almost like he was talking to himself. Rarely did he get any kind of lengthy response. Most of them would be only one or two syllables.

He opened his door and got out, waiting for Nadine, who followed meekly behind him as if she were still afraid he would abandon her. But she followed and picked up her speed as they approached the front door to the shop. Carefully, he opened it, and they entered the dark interior. Jackson held out his flashlight and cast the beam around, looking for any kind of unwelcome surprises that they might encounter. Thankfully, there was nothing. He advanced into the first aisle, picking up a wheeled cart on the way so that he could load it up. Nadine took one, and carrying the other small flashlight, she split from him to cover more ground.

Jackson headed for the back of the store where the food was more likely to be, and he took his arm to slide the available canned goods into his cart. Then, he wiped out the section with the chips in it. He saw a large case of bottled water and loaded it into the bottom of the cart before hurrying across to the shelf with the individually wrapped baked goods.

Nadine stayed at the front, and Jackson could hear her selecting items from the impulse shelves near the registers. She picked up more lip balm, some lighters, and some batteries for the flashlights. Then she took her cart to the first aid section. Although they might not need anything of that sort, she still grabbed bandages, braces, alcohol, sports tape, and anything else that might help with an injury. Of course, they also couldn't afford for either of them to become ill either, so she picked up some painkillers and cold medicine in as large quantities as she could manage, not sure when they would get a chance like this again. Then, as a noise rang out toward the rear of the store, a sound like metal screeching against the linoleum tile, she bolted for the car.

Jackson had his cart between himself and the skeleton, and he was trying to head for the door, but he was afraid to turn his back on the thing. He'd seen how fast they could move. Finally, he let go of the cart and reached for the gun in his belt, but the thing seemed to realize what he was doing. It lunged for him. He managed to fire one shot, but it struck the skeleton's torso and ricocheted off. Then, it clenched his arm in its metallic hand, his elbow being crushed by the skeleton as it tried to pull him toward it. He screamed in agony, unable to escape its grip. Blood began to seep from the wound. Then suddenly, the skeleton froze, its body illuminated by blue electrical light as Nadine held the stun gun to its head. She didn't stop, and Jackson fell to the floor, weakened by the loss of adrenaline. When Nadine had drained the stun gun, she finally dropped it, appearing satisfied that she had attacked one of them and won. For David.

She knelt down, even as the thing crashed against the tile, and helped Jackson to his feet. The current had stunned him, as well, but he came to as she tugged his good arm over her shoulders until he could stand. He leaned against the cart for support as he wobbled, feeling sharp pain as he tried to push it toward the door. Red blood dripped copiously onto the floor. Quickly, Nadine helped him walk to the front of the store where she had left her cart, and she opened a bottle of alcohol to cleanse the wound on Jackson's arm. He cried out as she poured the liquid over his arm, then wiped the blood off with gauze before covering it with a bandage. Without any first aid experience, she'd done the best she could. He was definitely grateful.

They took their carts out to the parking lot and emptied them into the trunk of the car, Nadine doing most of the heavy lifting. Then, she went back into the store for bags to carry their supplies to their next resting place, wherever that might be, while Jackson carefully climbed into the driver's seat. How was he going to drive? He worried about his pain level as he raised his arm to the wheel. But when Nadine returned and put the bags into the back, she brought him a couple of aspirin and a bottle of water before she went to her usual spot on the passenger's side.

"Thank you," he told her, feeling his arm shake as he took the pills. Thinking of the near miss, he knew he couldn't fight the skeletons hand-to-hand. There was no way. They were much stronger than people. What were he and Nadine going to do?

———

They huddled on the floor in a hotel room in a new town,

barricading the doors and the windows as they had done in another hotel in a town many miles away. Somehow, the room looked nearly identical. Jackson had his arm in a sling, resting it after the long drive. He was trying to eat with his good arm, but Nadine had to help him with the canned dinner before he could attempt to eat from a bag of chips. The room was like a darkened sauna, with not even the hum of air-conditioning to break the silence. The only sound was his crunching the chips, which started to annoy him.

"Talk to me," he asked her. He hoped she would oblige him this one time.

"What do you want me to say?" She didn't seem to have the same irritation at the soundless void that he had.

"I don't know. It's just too quiet."

She frowned. "I don't want to attract any of those things here."

He sighed. "No. I guess we don't." He stood and picked out a bottle of water from the pack they'd brought with them. Then he went to the bed and sat on the mattress, leaning against the headboard, feeling lost and like he'd already failed in every way imaginable. How could he fight against thousands of the skeletons with only one arm? He could feel the painkillers wearing off and wanted to take more, but he was afraid to use too many.

Nadine reached for a water and joined him on the bed, leaning back and sipping from it as if there were nothing wrong at all. She was always somber, but maybe that wasn't her true personality. She had a recent tragedy (as had everyone), and it was difficult to be cheerful under those circumstances.

Jackson gulped the water, feeling thirsty after his salty dinner. He wished he'd thought to bring a second bottle, but it hadn't occurred to him. Instead, he held the empty bottle and stared at the remaining drops as they spun around on the bottom as he moved his hand. A couple of them clung to the sides as if they were trying to save themselves. He didn't have the energy to throw the bottle away, much less grab another one. So, he put the cap on and lay down, unexpectedly feeling wiped out. Maybe it was blood loss. Maybe it was the adrenaline drain. He wasn't sure. But he wasn't sure he could even stay awake five more minutes. Slowly, he dozed, feeling the darkness envelop him like a warm blanket.

———————

When Jackson woke in the middle of the night, Nadine was sleeping beside him. Carefully, he put an arm down to assist him in sliding off the bed, but he felt pain shoot up to his shoulder. Inadvertently, he must have cried out because she woke suddenly, then she was at his side, helping him off the bed. He could have wept, feeling ashamed that he was almost incapacitated by a hurt arm. She let him go once he was free from the covers that he didn't remember having over him when he had gone to sleep, and he made his way to the bathroom to check his wounds. The covering gesture seemed out of character coming from her, as he hadn't thought she felt warmly enough toward him to show such an intimate sign of affection. Or maybe he was reading too much into it, he decided.

They'd left a flashlight in the small room because they could close the door, and the light couldn't be seen from outside. So, he set it on its side and slowly unwound the bandage, wincing as the cloth came unfurled and peeled a little off some of the scabs on his skin. Seeing the blood well up again made him feel sick. How long would it take to heal?

Would it become infected? If it did, how could he treat himself without a doctor or…what? He had no medical knowledge at all, and he didn't even know how to research the possible treatments for it without the internet. Would it even be safe to find a library? Angry at his situation, he cleaned the wound a little more roughly than he had intended to. The pain was good. He deserved it. This was stupid.

But then, he had no idea how to get the bandage back on. It was filthy and blood-soaked anyway, and he thought it best to clean it before using it again. Plugging the drain, he filled the sink with some water and alcohol before immersing the bandage, wishing they had some heat to complete the process. But he turned off the light before opening the door and looking in the bag with the medical supplies in it for a clean bandage. Nadine cleared her throat, and he looked up, only to see her holding a bandage up to the small light in her hand so that he could see it. Sheepishly, he sighed and walked over to her, allowing her to wrap his arm and thinking he could be much less stubborn, and it would help both of them.

"What do you think?" he said as she tucked in the end of the fabric and handed him the light. "Do you think we should stay here one more day? I want to get this done, but I also think I'm in no shape to do any fighting."

"I don't know. I'm scared to stay too long, but knowing where we're going doesn't make me want to get there any faster," she answered.

He had to admit she had a point. "Yeah."

She patted the bed next to her for him to sit down, and he sighed a little louder than he meant to. It was more about the pain than anything else, but she must have thought he was annoyed with her. She stood up and retreated to the other side of the bed, as she had done when he'd first rescued her. As a consolation, he picked up two bottles of water and carried one to her, sitting next to her against the headboard. She took the water but didn't comment.

"I'm sorry. It's my arm. Everything hurts it. I didn't mean anything," he explained.

She accepted this by nodding slightly. Then, she took his bottle of water and opened it, probably knowing he couldn't do so very easily. He hoped that meant everything would be fine between them. Thanking her as she handed it back, he wished he had a plan. All he knew was that he'd seen something that might hold a key, but he couldn't figure out how to use what he'd seen there to solve the problem. How could a bunch of artifacts show how to kill the skeletons or how to somehow disable them forever? He wasn't a scientist or researcher. What did he think he could accomplish?

Nadine suddenly gripped his hand tightly, her breath coming in shaky gasps as she nearly panicked. He'd heard nothing, but at her reaction, he thought he could hear something metallic in the distance. Quickly, he doused her light, and they sat as still and silently as they could. Jackson put his good arm around her, holding her close and trying to convey that they would be safe in that room. As long as they were quiet, they would be fine.

The sounds came closer, metallic clanging against concrete that came in smaller numbers than the first time they'd encountered the skeletons. However, they seemed to head straight for the hotel, surrounding it and circling it. Nadine almost started to whimper, but Jackson quickly held a hand to her mouth again, whispering in her ear that he was sorry, but he had to keep her quiet. She nodded in understanding but still shivered and cried while he embraced her.

Then came sounds like the front door was being tried below them. Jackson and Nadine had locked it and piled furniture against it, but Jackson knew the skeletons' strength. They could force it if they wanted to. He felt his own breath quicken in response, suddenly very afraid. Neither he nor Nadine dared to move. The gun was lying on the table across the room. Would it even do anything against the skeletons at all? He didn't want to chance getting up to grab it. It might not be worth it anyway. Remembering the way that the bullet he'd fired had ricocheted off the skeleton that had attacked him, he wondered what they could do to protect themselves from any of them.

Suddenly, the shuddering at the front door quietened, and they waited to see what the skeletons would try next. Would they force the door? Would they set fire to the hotel? What methods were permissible to them? Jackson hoped they had not determined anyone was inside, but it didn't take a great leap to figure it out. He felt his hand begin to tremble and wished he could control his feelings better, not wanting to transmit his fears to Nadine.

They listened intently for any sign that the skeletons might have entered the hotel, but there was nothing but metallic footsteps outside on the street. Slowly, the footsteps seemed to move away, as if the skeletons were now roaming the countryside for anyone they had not yet killed. Jackson wanted to protect Nadine now that he'd supposedly rescued her from the initial onslaught. But had he done her a favor at all? What terrifying new world had he rescued her into?

Waking in the hotel room in the middle of the afternoon, Jackson started abruptly, remembering the night before. Nadine was gone, and he panicked as if she'd disappeared forever, as if he might have just imagined the previous several days with her. The bathroom door opened, jolting him further, and he felt a tremendous relief wash over him at seeing her standing there.

She sat down at the table and took a can of something out of their supplies, and he tried to decide if he was hungry, also, or too disturbed to eat. Eventually, he thought it might calm him to sit with her, so he wiped the fatigue from his face and slid carefully off the bed. He used his good arm for support and then picked up the sling from where he'd left it draped on a chair the day before. Before he'd asked her to, Nadine had opened a can for him and set aside a fork for him to eat with, so he thanked her and ate it the best he could, bracing the can against the wall and the arm in the sling so that he could create a small amount of leverage against it with the fork. It took most of his concentration to manage it, but he was grateful for Nadine's presence, regardless.

After their feeble lunch, Nadine helped Jackson clean his arm and re-dress it. It looked slightly better, but the bruises had become more evident now that the puncture wounds were no longer bleeding and had started to heal. It wasn't much, though, and he worried how long it would be before he could fully use the arm again. How long would they be stuck there in that hotel, and how long would it be before they were found? He practiced moving the arm around in slow circles to keep it from locking up as it healed, but he didn't want to exert himself. Eventually, he found himself back on the bed asleep, as if he'd dreamed the whole morning.

Hearing Nadine's snoring, though, at least let him know she was beside him. He didn't bother moving. Part of him debated whether he should get up and eat something else or whether he should just go back to sleep. Another part of him said he desperately needed to use the shower. The shower won out, and he made his way into the bathroom, proud that he'd managed it without assistance, and he removed the bandage long enough to rinse off. When he walked back into the bedroom, Nadine was yawning and holding her arms out as if she already knew what he was going to ask her. He stood next to the bed so that she could rewrap his arm, then he picked out a bag of chips and a bottle of water, sitting at the table so that he might stay awake long enough to eat it.

"I think we should leave," he decided. "I don't want to be here when they come back tonight. There might be more of them."

Nadine sat stoically, staring into space. He wasn't sure if she'd heard him, but when he started to repeat himself, she said, "I don't either."

At first, he felt confused, not sure what she meant, but she stood and started to gather their belongings, what few of them they had, and packed them into their overnight bags. He wanted to help, but she had almost finished by the time he'd only put away a couple of items. Finally, she slung the heavier carry-on bag over her shoulder, leaving only the beach bag with her clothes in it for him to carry. Grateful for her foresight, he picked it up with the gun while she held the flashlight out to illuminate the building interior as they made their way down the hall.

They checked their barricades warily, hurrying downstairs and toward the back door. Jackson thought he heard a sound behind him, and he spun, seeing part of the barricade at the front door unfold itself into a metal skeleton with glowing red eyes. Nadine screamed, and Jackson fired the gun into the skeleton's head as he ran, the only target he could find in the black space behind him. Both of them heard a crash as they opened the rear door, but they didn't stop to see if Jackson's bullets had achieved their goal. Instead, they threw their bags into the back seat of the car while Jackson started the engine, feeling pain return to his arm as the initial shock wore off.

The car almost made a clean getaway. But before it had left the rear lot, the back door of the hotel flew open, and the skeleton was instantly at the vehicle's side, gripping the door handle and attempting to force it open. The window shattered, and glass pellets showered Jackson as he tried to hold onto the door, but Nadine's arm reached past him with another stun gun, lighting the skeleton up the way she'd done with the previous one and freezing it in place. Finally, she stopped the current and dropped the stun gun onto the floor while Jackson gunned the engine again and tried to leave. They heard the shrieking of metal and a grinding sound as the skeleton rebooted and gripped the bumper. Then, the car accelerated, leaving the thing hanging with the muffler until it dropped off into the road as they sped away, the roaring of the engine the only noise in the empty town.

Jackson drove into the next town with much trepidation. The engine sounds were deafening in the silent streets as he looked for a safe hiding place. He didn't think they would make it far in the damaged vehicle, but he didn't know how to hotwire a car anyway. They parked behind an old building that might have once been a bank, and then they ran across to an old apartment building next door. The building had once had a guard, but the station was bloodied and empty when they arrived. The blood must have been there for days as it didn't appear fresh, but there were no footprints or anything to indicate anyone had been there recently. They watched their own steps carefully and found keys to the individual apartments in the maintenance office, where Jackson chose one at random, only taking the time to make sure it was upstairs before they took the stairs to the upper levels.

Jackson opened the door quietly once they found the correct apartment, and he gestured for Nadine to wait in the hall while he checked it out. However, she didn't follow his suggestion and, instead, walked around the small flat with him, still holding the flashlight so that his hand was free to hold the gun.

Once they were sure it was empty, they locked the door and blocked it with the sofa and piled the heavy coffee table on top of it, as well. Or maybe it only seemed heavy because of his injured arm. Nadine seemed to have no trouble with it. Then, he sat at the dining table, sweating and in agony, while Nadine rifled through the cabinets and closets for more supplies.

When Nadine reappeared, he had his head down on the table with his arm resting in his lap to avoid straining it. Nadine had already drawn the blackout curtains and piled furniture in front of the windows in both the living room and the master bedroom. She had a new T-shirt on, a long pink thing with a sparkly design on the front, and the same cargo pants from before. The "new" T-shirt was a bit large on her, so he assumed the pants from the householder didn't fit her or she would have put them on. She handed him a couple of shirts and checked his arm to make sure it hadn't begun bleeding again before she picked out something to eat for both of them.

Jackson rose to refresh himself while she did so, and he washed his face with soap in the bathroom, taking a second to rinse out his hair and also to rid himself of any remaining glass pellets. Then, he changed into one of the shirts Nadine had given him. It said "Tommy Hilfiger" in large letters across the front, but it was definitely nicer than the one he'd been wearing previously.

Returning to the dining room, he saw Nadine sitting with the small light on, eating some sort of chicken and rice out of a can. There was a can in his vacated seat with a fork next to it, but she'd piled a couple of small kitchen appliances that he couldn't identify on the table behind the can so that he would have something to brace it against. "Thanks," he said as he sat down again.

"Was there any glass?" she asked him, perhaps worried about his proximity to the broken car window earlier.

He shook his head. "Not much. Nothing got in my eyes." He wanted to think she cared about him, but it was probably just because he'd been helping her, and without him, she'd be on her own. But how did he feel about *her*? Did he care about her? Well, of course, he did. He didn't feel he knew her any better than before, but they'd shared experiences, so maybe he had bonded with her to some degree.

They were now only a day or so from Smithton Lake. Stay here as long as possible to recuperate and to come up with a plan, he thought. It made sense. Trying to disable or destroy the skeletons was dangerous if he were fully able.

It would be worse now. He thought about the artifacts he'd seen and tried to remember what they actually looked like. Even the few days that had passed seemed more like years.

He remembered the lab and the leaded glass walls and doors and thought they could figure out how to gain entry one way or another. After that, he was unclear. Would they need some sort of equipment to analyze everything? If so, what would they need? He didn't want to stay anywhere for an extended period, afraid that would increase their chances of being found, but what if the equipment they needed to do any analysis was only present there in the lab? And what if they needed power to run it? That would be impossible without the grid being operational.

Realizing he was trapping himself in a hypothetical nightmare, he shook his head to clear it and looked up to see Nadine staring at him. "Is everything okay?" he asked her.

She shook her head slightly. "I don't know."

He tried not to feel frustrated at the lack of a real answer. "Is something wrong?"

"I'm just worried about when we get to Smithton Lake."

Well, he could see that was probably an issue. "Yeah. Me, too."

"Are you sure we have to go there?" she pleaded quietly.

"We already talked about this," he argued.

"You weren't hurt then," she pointed out.

She was right, but he didn't like it. "I know, but I can't keep driving forever, and I don't want to be worrying about those skeleton things for the rest of my life, however long that is. I want to *know* they're gone. Do you understand?"

She nodded, but she seemed unsure.

"Do you understand?" he asked again. "I'm not sure you realize how exhausted I am. I'm not sure there *is* a place safe from those things. We could keep driving until the end of time, and we might still be hiding. I don't want to do that anymore. I can't. I just can't."

"I don't want to die," she cried.

He empathized, but he disagreed. "I don't either. I don't think that's what this means at all."

"What if we can't stop them? What if we die in the attempt? We could, you know?"

He rubbed his temples, trying to ease the strain. "I know. Yes, we could. But we might not. It's the only chance we have to really be free."

"I don't want to die," she repeated.

"We might not die," he corrected her.

She shuddered and set aside her canned dinner. "I'm happy that you're confident, but I'm not. I'm scared."

"I know you are. I'm scared, too," he admitted. "I will try to plan this to minimize any risk. I really don't want to die, either."

She sighed lightly, standing to gather some of the bottles of water. She opened one and handed it to Jackson before sitting with the other. "Before, we thought your car could make it up to the building. Do you still think it could do that?"

"Er…no. I didn't want to think about that."

"I don't either, but I don't want to do anything dangerous for no reason. If we can't get to the building, it's pointless." She crossed her arms as if daring him to contradict her.

"We'll figure out how to hotwire a car," he suggested.

She looked doubtful. He was tired of her skepticism but didn't want to antagonize her. "We'll figure it out," he assured her.

She nodded, but she seemed to be withdrawing from the conversation, so he decided to drop it. Planning was important, but he hoped they had plenty of time. He hoped they were safe for a few days, at least. However, he didn't want to assume.

He stood from the table and walked down the short hall to the bedroom. It was nearly black with the barricade. "Thanks for your help with this," he told her honestly.

Nadine still looked surly, but she accepted his words and finally stood up to follow him. It wasn't late, but they knew the sun was going down. The master bedroom in the apartment was larger than the bedrooms in some of the hotels they'd stayed in. It held a king-size bed, which felt almost like an unnecessary luxury, as did the Egyptian cotton sheets and pillowcases. It was too hot to sleep under the downy blankets, but Jackson and Nadine felt comfortable on top of the quilt regardless. Jackson wanted to stretch out on the humongous mattress, but Nadine surprised him by curling up next to him, still not touching. It was the first time he realized that it was intentional and not just because they had to share a smaller bed. He felt guilty that he'd upset her earlier and that he'd not been more understanding. Although she was turned away from him, he knew she was thinking about their predicament and how to get out of it. He figured he would be awake thinking about it, too.

————

CHAPTER
EIGHT

It had been a few days, and Jackson felt he needed to do something toward their end goal. His arm was still in the process of healing, but he'd stopped wearing the sling by then. He and Nadine were outside in the parking lot down the street. Jackson held the two wires together, hoping to hear the engine catch, but absolutely nothing happened. Nadine kept watch, periodically using a damp hand towel to wipe the sweat from his eyes while he tried to solve the dilemma of the moment.

First, they'd tried to find the resident's keys to the apartment, hoping there would also be vehicle keys. However, the resident must have fled because there were no such things anywhere. Then, Jackson found a tool kit in a closet, and they began tearing up vehicles' steering columns and dashboards, trying to figure out how to start them without a key. He, again, wished for a library, but he didn't think they had time to do any research anyway. There weren't old-style card catalogs anymore. He wasn't even sure there were microfiche machines, not that those were helpful as they still relied on the power grid to work. Modern technology was a weakness.

After the fourth failure, Jackson cursed and shook his head. "Maybe you were right. Maybe this is a bad idea. I'm not cut out to be a car thief."

"Let's go upstairs and rest awhile," she suggested. They hadn't gone far from the apartment building, and they hurried back inside, hoping they hadn't been observed. Jackson went into the bedroom once they were back upstairs and had re-barricaded the door. He wished he could just sit on the sofa, but that was the heaviest item they had besides an armoire that was much too monstrous to move. Nadine joined him shortly after, bringing two bottles of water with her. Jackson's was already open, and he swallowed it almost in one gulp, exhausted and dehydrated from the heat and the wasted effort. Nadine lay back on the bed after drinking hers, having replaced the cap so that the remainder wouldn't spill.

He looked over at her and wished she had an answer for him. Lying back next to her, he closed his eyes briefly, not sure if he wanted to sleep for a while or just to sit in the darkness for a few minutes. His head hurt from so much exertion in the blazing sun, but he didn't have the energy to collect another bottle of water.

Was there a solution he hadn't thought of? He was sure that if he thought about it enough, something would occur to him, but he was so tired from the heat and lack of proper nutrition that he could barely think straight at all. What if he just replaced the muffler on his car? No, that still wouldn't work. He didn't know the first thing about auto repair, he reminded himself. Mufflers came in all sorts of different shapes and sizes. How would he know which one to use? And would it just rattle around without the bumper there? He wasn't sure. But announcing their arrival in Smithton Lake with a large cloud of black exhaust didn't sound safe to him either.

He heard a light buzzing sound, thinking that maybe an insect had managed to get past them into the apartment before he realized it was Nadine's snoring. Surely, he needed to prove to her that he could fix the problem he'd brought her into. Then again, maybe she had the answer herself. She had yet to suggest it, but she might figure the whole thing out before long, he hoped. He had to realize that not everything was up to him. He'd been treating her like an accessory, almost, and he hadn't meant to. However, she hadn't really spoken to him much about anything except very briefly. She rarely revealed anything about herself, and he wasn't even convinced that everything she'd told him was true. That she'd lost someone was clear. But what about everything else? *What else, though?* She'd revealed very little.

He took a deep breath, then turned onto his side, away from the recovering arm, so that he could take a nap. Yes, sleep on it. Maybe his dreams would divulge the answer. If not, he would ask Nadine in the morning.

———

They walked the streets of the small town, carrying a small bag of weapons for protection. Jackson still held the handgun, but Nadine had selected one of the larger machine guns and slung it over her shoulder like a guerrilla. It was scary that it didn't faze him at all anymore.

They didn't speak, only communicating with hand gestures to indicate what they wanted to do. When they reached the main street, Jackson pointed emphatically at the building ahead of him, and Nadine grinned happily at their stroke of luck. Hurrying across the road, they went inside the office at the auto garage they'd spotted, looking for a completed ticket that showed the work was done with a vehicle description and a key. There was one ticket still there. The sedan parked outside behind the shop was fixed, and they both went out to look at it, hoping it wasn't an electric car and, therefore, inoperable. It was nondescript and silver, a color that would blend into the road at almost all times of day, thankfully. He tried the key, which had been in the pouch with the ticket in the office, and it opened the door, so he sat in the driver's seat and attempted to start it. The engine purred. He let out his breath and shared a rare smile with Nadine. Then, he gestured for her to get inside, and they drove the car down the street and parked it next to theirs at the bank, where they both transferred their belongings that hadn't been brought upstairs with them.

Relieved, they went back upstairs, covering each other with their weapons, still not letting down their guard even as they reached the familiar territory. After they had checked out the place and replaced their barricade against the door, Jackson sat at the dining table, smiling at Nadine again. "What a relief that I don't have to steal a car," he told her.

"You did steal that car," she corrected him.

He frowned. "Yeah, I guess that's still stealing."

She smiled slightly, handing a bottle of water to him across the table as she sat down. "I forgive you," she said.

He shook his head, unsure if she was joking. "I'm sure it's a relief that you don't have to wait for me to figure out how to hotwire anything."

"That could take a very long time," she replied, straight-faced.

Puzzled, he looked at her, and then she burst into quiet giggles, so used to being silent that she couldn't even laugh at full volume when amused. He shook his head again but gave her a grin before sipping his water. "Does this mean you approve of the rest of my plan?"

She quietened and sighed. "I'm not sure."

"We should be able to leave tomorrow, I would think. My arm is getting better, but I don't know if we should wait. We've been lucky so far, but I don't want to wait until we're found to flee."

"I don't want to be found at all."

"Obviously," he agreed.

"Okay. We'll rest tonight and leave tomorrow," she said, reluctant.

He knew she wasn't happy with his plan. He didn't like it either. Nothing was certain. What could they do without knowing what they would find at the lab?

———

Coming into the lake area from another direction was slightly disorienting but not unsettling. What was unsettling was the massive dome-like structure that was now sitting above the lake. It had long legs, almost like stilts, that kept it from touching the water. And there was a high-pitched whine they could feel as much as hear that pervaded the entire area around the lake. They had felt it getting louder the closer they approached until the lake was visible over the hill. Jackson paused the car, now rethinking his plan. Would they be spotted more easily in the car? What if they had already been seen?

He looked at the structure, trying to discern its purpose. It had angular features that resembled the skeletons, but it had no windows of any kind. He couldn't see if there were any version of the skeletons' eyes that might apply to the larger frame, but he saw nothing to indicate that there was any sort of surveillance. However, he wondered if there was sonic technology, like radar, or anything that might be tied into the whining noise…anything at all that might give away their existence or location.

"Erm…this changes things quite a bit," he whispered.

"Why? What does it mean?" Nadine asked.

"I don't know. What do you think? I'm afraid they'll see us or hear us or something. I don't know what that noise is. What if it's not just an engine noise?"

"What else would it be?"

He didn't want to scare her, but he didn't want to hide it from her, either. "I'm not sure. But what if it has multiple purposes, or if they can use it to sense when something is moving out here?"

"They'll know we're coming?" She looked alarmed.

"I don't know. But now, I'm not as confident about driving up to the lab. Maybe they've even been there already."

"So, what are we going to do?" She looked terrified then, and she was visibly trembling as if she were about to start crying again.

He slowly pulled the car back behind the hill, then turned off the engine. He'd had to look past her to see the lake, and he looked from the distance back to her again. "I'm sorry, Nadine."

"For what?"

"For making the wrong decisions. For getting us into a bigger mess."

Tears fell from her eyes, and he fought the impulse to wipe them away. He sighed. Then, he slumped in his seat, feeling defeated. What else could he do? What did he need to do to fight the skeletons? Did he now need to destroy the structure above the lake? What if it was completely irrelevant? Was there anything that could be done, at this point, anyway?

He covered his face with his hands. At first, he was just going to wipe away some exhaustion, but then, he felt the weight of everything they had been through over the last few days, the weight of all the decisions he'd made that had led them here and into a potentially gruesome end. He didn't want to lose control of himself in front of Nadine, but he could hardly control it. Partly, he felt like screaming out in anger, but he managed to dial it down slightly to a few angry tears, then he took a few ragged breaths to calm himself. Looking over at Nadine to gauge her reaction, he thought she looked frightened.

He gave her a sad smile. "I'm sorry. I just…I don't know what to do now." A few more tears threatened to escape, and he turned away so she couldn't see them.

"I don't know," she said. "Maybe we need to get out to that thing on the lake instead of the lab?"

He shook his head, still not turning back from the window. "I doubt it would be as simple as it looks from here."

"It doesn't look simple from here."

"My point exactly."

She sighed. "We have to do something. We came all this way."

He took a deep breath, then turned back to her. "I know. I think that's the most logical thing, but I don't know how to do it. It might be best to go during the day, but what will we do tonight. I don't know if we'll have time to plan anything and also get to execute it before darkness falls."

She seemed to shiver.

"We need to find a shelter of some sort, and then we'll figure out what to do. I don't want to do this the wrong way," he said.

She shook her head. "Where can we possibly stay? We're not safe here."

Jackson looked around and decided he should stay out of sight of the lake. He turned the engine back on and backed down the hill slightly until he reached a turn for a driveway. Taking the car down the drive, he pulled into the garage of a lake house that looked dark and empty. There wasn't another

car, and he took one of the automatic rifles as he got out of the
sedan and closed the garage door. In the darkness, he took
out the flashlight and used it to find the door to the interior,
which he hoped wasn't locked. It wasn't. The occupants may
have left in a hurry. He searched through the house just in
case, with Nadine behind him, also armed. The house wasn't
overly large and wasn't any cooler than any of the hotels or
the apartment from the nights before, but there was no sign
of anyone, not even in the closets or the attic. Jackson took the
time to return to the car and lock the garage door. Then, he
took their bags and went to barricade the doors and windows
of the house with the furniture as they'd done everywhere
they'd stayed. He wasn't sure how secure it would be, but
he hoped it would still look deserted or they would, at least,
have some warning if anyone or any*thing* tried to enter.

Jackson took out a couple of cans of food and some
plastic ware. "Do you want to eat something? We'll see what
we can work out while there's still some daylight left."

She sat down and took one of the cans reluctantly. She
didn't seem very excited about eating, and he knew she was
tired of cold canned goods. He was, too.

They both took a few bites, thinking. Then, Jackson
realized how tired he was and how much they had both been
through. He wanted to sleep again. But he knew they didn't
have time. They had to come up with a plan. They discussed
different ways of getting out to the structure, but they couldn't
see, from their vantage point, if there was anything that would
be considered an entrance. Maybe they would just have to
make their own. But there had to be a way to get inside. If it
was related to the skeletons' technology, then they wanted to
know what it was doing there.

They were afraid that if they got out to the structure and it turned out to be pointless, they would have announced their presence to any skeletons nearby, and they would probably be dead. Just in case, they planned for that eventuality, too.

Part of the plan was that they figured there would be a speedboat nearby. With a lake as large as that one, surely there would be people who owned one somewhere. Hopefully, they weren't all locked up. However, although Jackson was still afraid it would be too noisy, he thought they should try to use speed to gain entrance rather than take longer to get to the structure with a quieter boat. They would use the boat to get out to the structure and then use their weapons to gain entrance if they could. From there, it would depend on what they found, but they tried to plan different scenarios.

Finally, Jackson had enough. "We'll finish this tomorrow." He wiped his eyes and then headed for the bedroom.

Nadine followed him. "You don't have to share the same room," he said, looking back. "I think there is another one if you want some privacy."

She shook her head. "I don't want to be alone. What if they find us?"

He wanted to argue but didn't think he could convince her she was safe if he wasn't sure himself. Instead, he just nodded his consent and carefully set the gun down next to the wall before crawling into the bed. She copied his actions and then climbed in next to him. He heard her sigh as he turned the flashlight out and tried to conserve the batteries.

"I'm sorry this turned out the way it did. I wish I could have...." He didn't know how to finish his statement.

"I know. I didn't have any better ideas, though."

"Maybe not, but I wanted to help you, not put you in harm's way again."

She was quiet for a moment, and he thought, at first, that she had fallen asleep. "No. It's okay. I need to do something. Those skeletons took my life away that night. They took away everything that had mattered to me. I need to do this. I need to stop them, too."

"We all lost something that night," he agreed.

———

The hum intensified overnight. They could hear what sounded like thousands of the skeletons on the roads outside, but they couldn't tell what was going on without peeking through the windows. They wanted to stay hidden. It sounded like some of the skeletons came into the grounds around the house, but most of them didn't seem to pause. They walked fairly quickly, as if with a purpose. Jackson and Nadine were afraid the purpose involved coming into the house, and the skeletons came very close to the windows. Although some of them paused outside the bedroom window, they did not try to enter. Hopefully, Jackson and Nadine thought, the skeletons assumed the house was still empty.

With the hum that much louder, it was harder to relax and sleep. Jackson wanted to see what the lake structure was doing to cause the hum to increase in volume, of course, but didn't dare go out to the road to look. Instead, he put his arm around Nadine, who was shivering and tried his best to be comforting. It would be fine. They would be fine.

———

Hours later, the noise seemed to subside slightly. The number of skeletons outside seemed to diminish, although Jackson and Nadine could still hear some of them in the distance. They tried to get a small amount of sleep after the rough night, but it was difficult. They still feared being discovered, but they wanted to be rested for their excursion later that day.

Jackson had serious doubts about going out to the facility over the lake, but he had no idea what else they could do. He wasn't sure that going to the lab was a better plan either, so he felt conflicted. Would either plan matter anyway? Was this pointless and futile to attempt? He just wanted to stop the skeletons. He almost didn't care how, but now he didn't want any harm to come to Nadine in the process. What if he lost her? How would he cope with being alone? He tried to push the thought out of his mind, but he was having trouble falling asleep in his anxiety.

Eventually, he managed to sleep for a couple of hours. Afraid to sleep much longer, he didn't want to waste too much of the day. Even though he didn't know why the skeletons seemed more active at night, he didn't care. He only hoped it increased Nadine's and his chances of making it across the lake safely if there weren't any of the skeletons about. That was the theory, anyway.

He groggily got out of bed and made his way to the bathroom, where he performed a very quick version of his morning routine. Sadly, he used the flashlight to shave, thinking the goatee was too difficult to maintain without proper lighting and splashed some water onto his face to wake up. Then, he went back into the bedroom, leaving the flashlight behind for Nadine. She woke upon hearing him open the door, and he gestured that she could use the bathroom, but then he realized that she probably couldn't see the hand motion in the darkness. She stood up slowly and made her way to the room, regardless.

While she was gone, he lay back on the bed and tried not to fall asleep again. The heat was making him feel more exhausted, however. He wiped his eyes and tried to focus on what they were going to do. But what *were* they going to do? Was it best to go with the new plan? What if they were spotted? What would happen, then? Would going across slowly be any better? Quieter, maybe. But "better" was a relative term. Was "quieter" better than "quicker"? He wasn't sure.

He started when he heard the door open and realized he'd dozed briefly. Or he hoped it was briefly. She brought the flashlight with her, thankfully, so he took it in search of some food, and they ate their usual canned breakfast less than enthusiastically. He looked forward to living in a world without the skeletons so they could grow vegetables in a garden and cook fresh food, probably over a fire. At least until humans could work together and restore the grid, should there be any other survivors. However, he was aware that it might take generations for that to happen.

Jackson and Nadine packed up extra cans from the pantry in the house for later, just in case they had to flee. Then, they found some overnight bags, packed up, and carried the pre-loaded weapons and extra ammunition outside in search of a boat. They went out the back door and down toward the lake, trying to stay hidden by trees and any other obstacles. Jackson supposed they would go with whichever kind of boat they found that they were able to start, although his first choice was something that was fairly small and wouldn't be as easily visible.

Nothing was nearby or where they could gain access easily, however. A few boats were visible but not easily accessible. But those were too large to move to the water, or else they didn't look to be in good condition. Some were locked up, and Jackson didn't want to attract attention by attempting to destroy the locks. Frustrated, he and Nadine returned to the lake house to alter their plan. What now?

———————

CHAPTER NINE

"We'll be found!" Nadine cried.

"What are we supposed to do then?" Jackson snapped. "We're stuck here if we don't do something."

Sulking, Nadine turned away from him at the table, but he could hear her chewing her pastry lightly as if she were barely interested anymore.

He sighed heavily. "If you have a suggestion, I would really like to hear it about now," he told her honestly. Upon receiving no response, he wanted to shout that he didn't have all the answers, that perhaps she should try to help instead of simply criticizing everything he did. But that wouldn't solve anything. "I know you don't know what to do. I don't either, but if we work together, we might have a better chance at figuring this out."

She turned back slightly, still not facing him, but not completely away either. Maybe she was listening, maybe she wasn't. He rubbed his eyes and tried not to let his lack of sleep cause him to lose his temper. "It's not your fault," he continued. "I'm not mad at you. I just feel lost. I wish I knew what to do."

Nadine set her pastry wrapper on the table and slumped in her chair. "No. I don't suppose you do." Was it *another* criticism? He could barely believe it.

"Do *you* know?" he asked again, still feeling irritated and not being able to contain it fully. He was challenging her, though, and he didn't like it.

She simply frowned and shook her head.

He bit his lip and tried to dial back any anger he felt. It wouldn't help the situation. In fact, he might end up screaming at her if he didn't deal with it, and then they would probably give away their location and both end up dead. Looking back at her, he noticed a slight wetness on one of her cheeks and worried he'd made her cry. Really. Get it together, he told himself.

"Okay, let's start over," he began. "Maybe we should head out around the lake in the car. We might find something else we can use. The lake is huge. There has to be a marina or something somewhere. What do you think?"

Her hand went to her cheek as if trying to wipe any tears before he could see them. Then, she nodded and sat up straighter.

"Let's see if there's a map or an atlas or something around here. If not in this house, we can check a gas station," he suggested.

Both of them stood, searching the house's drawers and cabinets and closets and coming up empty. Reluctantly, Jackson picked up the car keys and held them up, indicating they should leave. Darkness would come soon enough. They didn't have a lot of time.

They cleared the door and checked to see that the garage was still unoccupied, holding weapons at the ready before hurrying out to the car. Then, they both climbed in, and Jackson turned the key to start the engine. He always felt some anxiety that it wouldn't start or that it would be very loud, but this car was quieter than his old one, so he was relieved. He took the car down the empty driveway and out to the street, then he drove away from the house, hoping they couldn't be seen from the structure over the water.

As soon as they saw a gas station about a mile down the road, they stopped and nervously went inside. Luckily, there were maps on a spinning display by the register, and Jackson took a couple of them before deciding that he should probably fill the gas tank while they were there. The longer they were there, the greater the risk, but he quickly found the release and went back to the car, with Nadine filling bags with more first aid supplies and food while he refueled the car. She was finished before he was, and he watched her put the bags in the back before he set the handle back in its cradle on the pump.

He drove the car around behind the building, parking in a space hidden from the road, although there was no way to tell from where they were if anything was hiding in the trees. Handing one map to Nadine, he unfolded the other and found the road that circled the lake, putting his finger on the line and tracing it around until he found something he'd never noticed on his previous trips to the area: a military base.

"Here. We can start here. I know it's not a marina, but maybe there are some other things we can use there," he said hopefully.

"There will be boats," Nadine told him.

He made a face. "Of course. I know that, but I'm thinking we might stock up on grenades or something, too. I'm not sure how much good the guns will do. I shot the one that attacked me, and the bullet just bounced off."

She just shrugged as if it didn't matter anymore. But he knew better by now. She was just upset and didn't want to tell him.

"What's wrong now?" he asked.

"Nothing." She stared straight ahead, not looking anywhere but at the tree line. He thought she might be trying to ignore him, but it was impossible with the two of them in such close proximity.

"What do you suggest? Do you want to go somewhere

else instead?" His tone was sharp.

"No. I don't." She folded her map and put it inside the glove box with the handgun she usually used, then she crossed her arms and sat there as if waiting.

He sighed heavily. This was tedious. "I'm not trying to argue with you. I'm just stressed out and tired. I really do want to know what you think."

Nadine didn't react. She sat there as if she hadn't heard him, and he wondered if she had the ability to tune him out.

"Nadine," he called. Nothing. "Nadine." He tried to gather his thoughts to put them into intelligible sentences. "I want to ask you something."

Finally, she turned to face him, but she said nothing.

"Do you hate me?" he managed to say. It came out sounding weak and like he might begin to weep, but he meant it more as if seeking an honest judgement. Hopefully, she didn't think he was fishing for compliments.

"No," she replied quietly. "No. I don't hate you."

Well, that was a relief. "I know you didn't...well, you probably never would have asked to go out with me or anything. We're very different. But I'd like to think that we can work together and that we make a good team most of the time. I don't want you to think I don't like you. I'm just not...I'm more easily frustrated when I'm tired, which is all the time now. Just don't think it's you because it's not."

Staring at her hands, she twisted them and fiddled with her thumbs. Eventually, she looked up at him and pursed her lips. "I'm sorry. I don't want to add to your stress. I wish I knew what to do." Her hand pushed a strand of her hair back from her face. "I'm tired, too. I want to stop them, but I'm scared."

"Okay, but that just means we have to do this soon. The sooner we stop them, the sooner we can rest. We can do this." He tried to sound optimistic and like he was sure they would succeed.

A curt nod was her only response, an affirmative reply that she would be ready. He put the car in gear again and followed the road, turning off when he reached a fork and heading away down a dirt and gravel path that seemed less a road than a hiking trail. Not sure what they would find, he wondered if they might even shelter there, but when they reached the end, a high gate of chain link blocked their progress. Jackson got out and walked to the guard house, but the guard had obviously left long before. He tried to open the door to the small room, but it was bolted shut, and he hadn't the strength to bust it down with his injured arm. The gate was stuck in the closed position, and he tried to push it out of the way to no avail.

He could easily have rammed it with the car, but that would obviously damage the car, and then they would be in the same position as before. Not knowing what else to try, he went back to his seat and sat with his head resting against the wheel. "What are we going to do?" he mumbled.

"Shoot the lock?" Nadine suggested. She didn't sound confident.

"No. We'll make too much noise. Do you think we can both shove the gate open?" He looked up, worried they'd already been there too long for safety.

She shrugged but got out of the car and headed for the gate. He followed, then he put both hands against the metal and braced his legs against the small guard house for more leverage. They succeeded in getting the frame off the track but didn't do much more. Jackson groaned in frustration.

When he looked back at Nadine, she was walking back to the car, and he thought she'd given up already. He was about to say something, but she only unlocked the trunk and then pulled out the bolt cutters from the toolbox they'd recovered at the apartment. Smiling, she walked back to the chain link and snipped a few of the wires until there was a large enough hole that they could both crawl through.

Jackson wanted to argue. He didn't want to walk around the whole base and would have preferred to bring the car, but he didn't know what else to do. So, he shrugged and crawled through behind her as she ran across the asphalt and concrete ahead of him in the direction of the lake. Their only hope was to find a boat. Anything else was a bonus.

———

They explored the base as quietly and quickly as they could, being unable to access the secured buildings or most of the vehicles. Almost everything was locked, and Jackson was loathed to search any of the bodies they encountered for keys or passes because of the smell. It had been several days since all of the soldiers had died, and there were flies and such surrounding what remained of the bodies to the extent that it was difficult to get near them. Jackson tried once but gagged so hard that he eventually threw up a few feet away.

Nadine stayed as far away as she could, as if she were having flashbacks from David's murder at the hands of the strangers. It felt like years ago that he'd rescued her, but also like it had only just happened. The dismembered bodies were horrific and frightening on their own but having seen the same thing happen right in front of her, he knew it was even more traumatic for Nadine. He did his best to spare her, but it was obvious that the skeletons (or whatever they really were) had considered the soldiers a threat. Perhaps they'd attacked there first and come into the lab complex immediately after. Jackson only knew that he didn't feel any better about seeing the unfortunate men and women dead on the base than Nadine did.

Nearing the lake, they found exactly what they were looking for. There were boats, some of them with armaments. Jackson knew he would have difficulty piloting the larger ones, so he mostly examined the smaller ones. There was room for cargo, and Jackson thought that would work for what they wanted it to do. However, then there was the problem of how to get it back to the lake house or what to do with it from there. Sighing again, Jackson wished he had been able to get the car inside, as he could have sent Nadine back to the house in it. But sending her walking through the base again on her own was unconscionable, especially on foot. He couldn't do it.

"Now what?" he asked her, hoping for some advice. Wiping his forehead from the heat and humidity, he leaned back against the wall of the building behind him. Nadine stared at the boat as if it held the answer.

Then, Jackson turned and saw that she wasn't looking at the boat at all but in the distance. "What's 'EMP'?" she wondered aloud.

He perked up immediately. "Electromagnetic pulse." Standing up straight again, he walked in the direction she'd been staring, seeing the letters "EMP" stamped on the side of what looked almost to be a bomb several thousand yards away. They both ran closer and closer until they were able to examine the thing and determine that it was, indeed, a bomb of some sort. It was encased in a metal harness that secured it to a trailer so it wouldn't roll off during transport. A large Humvee sat nearby as if the trailer had been meant for it, but it never got assembled.

"Let's see if that has any fuel," Jackson said of the Humvee. Nadine looked skeptical, but she waited while he climbed into the driver's seat to look for the keys. They were still in the ignition, but it started up when he turned it over. Relieved, he checked the gas gauge, only to see that it had about half a tank left. He slowly reversed until the trailer was almost touching, then turned it off. "Can you help me hook that up?" he requested.

She didn't say a word but walked over to the hitch and pulled at it, but it didn't move at all.

"There's a jack underneath there. It looks like they were trying to attach the trailer when...well, just raise it up a little. I'll reverse, but you'll have to guide me." He watched out the window of the Humvee, hoping she'd give him a little more in the way of directions.

Shrugging, she quickly maneuvered the jack and lifted the trailer, then waved her hands right or left for Jackson to see in the mirrors while he backed the vehicle into position. Then, she held her hands up high for him to stop, and he turned off the ignition, climbing down to help. But she already had the draw bar pinned before he could figure out what to do next. He'd forgotten she'd been living on a farm.

"Er...yeah. Thanks." He tried to think of what to do about the other car, but maybe they didn't need it if they had the Humvee. However, he knew the gas mileage would be better in the passenger car, especially if it wasn't trailing a giant bomb behind it.

"What do you want this for?" she asked as she circled around it.

"Those skeleton things. Bullets haven't always worked against them, but your stun guns did, for the most part. Maybe we just need a really *big* stun gun," he suggested.

"Will this stop all of them?"

He cleared his throat slightly. "Hmm. I'm not sure. Probably not, but it will take out all of them near Smithton Lake."

"How do you know?" She paced slightly, worrying about something that she didn't make apparent.

"Nuclear bombs. They knock out electrical systems nearby. This is supposed to do that without the actual 'bomb' part. Just the electromagnetic pulse. It won't harm us, but those skeletons look mechanical, don't they?"

Still thinking, she didn't answer right away. She continued to walk around as if it calmed her somehow. "We need to stop *all* of them. How will this do that?"

"I don't know, but I'm not sure we can afford *not* to take it. This might be our only chance to, at least, knock out several thousand of them."

"We need more," she insisted, and he wasn't sure he'd heard her properly.

"How? I'm not sure there *are* more of these. And we can't get into the buildings to see." He rubbed his face, taking his shirt to wipe some of the sweat out of his eyes. "Let's get out of here, and we'll discuss this on the way back. I don't feel safe here. Do you?"

She shook her head, and he climbed back into the Humvee, waiting for her to go around to the other side. Once she was in the passenger's seat, he started the engine again, then drove back the way they'd come. He hoped he could open the gate from inside the base, but it wasn't immediately clear how he would do that without a pass or key.

"Check the glove box," he said eventually.

She opened it, but there wasn't anything of interest. He had thought it was worth a try. Then, reaching the gate, he paused and looked around, climbing down and walking back to the guard house. His bolt cutters were still in the car, so he squeezed back through the hole in the chain link and picked them up. However, the lock on the guard house wasn't a padlock, and he couldn't just cut it. Great.

He didn't want to try to cut a hole large enough for the Humvee and trailer, so he shook his head, wandering the site and hoping something would present itself.

"Ram it with the car?" Nadine asked.

"We won't be able to drive the car. The mileage is better," he countered.

"We need this one. We don't need the car," she argued.

"We need both," he continued, unrelenting. "I don't know what's going to happen, and I'd rather we didn't lose the quiet one."

She sat back in her seat and leaned her head on her hand, her elbow against the window. Thinking he might chance ramming it with the Humvee instead, another thought occurred to him. Squeezing back through the hole, he went to the back of the larger vehicle and searched the trunk, finding a crowbar underneath the floorboard in the trunk. He took it victoriously through the hole once more, then shoved the bar into the door of the guard house and forced it open. He couldn't help but throw a grin toward Nadine as he released the lock on the gate, although the power had long since gone out, so it didn't retract. However, he was able to slide it to the side and then drive the Humvee out to the dirt road.

"Do you want to follow me in that one?" he asked Nadine, pointing to the passenger car.

"Not really," she complained.

"Do you want to drive this one, and I'll drive the other car?" he asked, trying not to snap at her.

Shrugging, she waited for him to jump down before sliding across to the driver's seat. Then, he wondered if that might be better anyway. She might have more experience driving with a trailer than he had.

"Back to the lake house, then park behind the house."

"They'll see it," she disagreed.

"Do you have a better idea? It won't fit in the garage," he said.

"We'll put the bomb in the garage, and everything else can sit in the driveway."

He didn't feel like fighting with her, so he nodded, and then he returned to the sedan and found the keys, starting it up and following slowly behind her as she took the trailer along the long, dirt road.

———

"Maybe we should have taken the boat," Nadine argued when they were inside the house. It was getting dark, and Jackson would have preferred she didn't shout.

"The bomb was too heavy for the boat. We'll figure something out," he said in a stage whisper, hinting to her that she needed to be quieter.

She threw her hands up and spun around, heading for the bedroom. Not knowing what else to do, he followed her, but he lay down on the bed heavily and stared at the ceiling, wondering what he was doing. Nadine was taking her clothes off in the bathroom, changing into something a little cleaner after their ordeal at the military base earlier. He wanted to do the same but was too tired to bother.

When she returned, she curled up on the mattress, close to him, although not as close as usual. He knew she was upset, and he started to think that maybe everything that was getting to him might be getting to her, as well. She wasn't living in a vacuum any more than he was. Maybe it wasn't even about the boat at all. He wanted her to be involved, thinking that would help her to feel like she had some control over the situation, but she didn't usually seem to want to offer suggestions at all. When she did, he usually didn't want to go along with them, so there was that. Perhaps that's why she rarely suggested anything, he thought to himself.

Part of him thought to apologize, but he barely knew what he was apologizing for. Perhaps it was just that he didn't listen very well, but he knew she could also be more vocal if she really wanted him to hear her. However, how was it her fault that he was so stubborn? Would it matter if she persisted in arguing, or would he just shut her down the way he usually did regardless?

Then again, maybe it had nothing to do with him at all. Maybe she was feeling lost that her boyfriend was dead, and she was stuck with a stranger she barely knew in the middle of an apocalypse that she could definitely do without. Maybe she would rather be facing her potential doom with someone she loved and not with him. He could relate to some degree. It wasn't as though this would be the way he'd want it to go, either.

Feeling slightly depressed, he didn't know how to

improve her mood and didn't want her to go to sleep upset. However, there wasn't anything he could say that would make it all better. It was the way it was. He turned over on the mattress, which didn't have Egyptian cotton bedding, but was still nicer than the old hotels. The sheets had a high thread count that made them opulently soft. He'd probably never have noticed if he hadn't gone without for so long, however.

Facing her, he could see that she had turned her back to him, but he could also tell from her breathing that she was not yet asleep. "What do you want me to do? I'm sorry if I'm not the best companion. I want to do better. I do. But I can't bring back David, and I don't know what else you'd like me to do."

Her breathing changed as if she'd tensed up, and he knew she'd heard him, but he wished her reaction had not been one of hostility. It made him feel terrible about how he'd treated her and about what he was like as a person. Did his words help or hurt things between them? Of course, he felt he wasn't the right person to help her grieve her loss anyway. She needed someone warmer and more approachable.

"What can I do to make things easier for you?" he added. "I wish I was different and/or that there was someone else here instead of me. But I care, even if it doesn't seem like it at times."

Finally, she flipped onto her back and sighed deeply. "It's not you. I don't want to do this anymore. I wish this was done so that we could just go on with our lives. I hate those things for what they did. But I don't want to keep doing this forever either, and I don't like that the plans keep changing, and I don't know what's going on."

He sat there, somehow stunned and unexpectedly

devastated by her words. Did she mean to leave him alone forever when they'd done what they'd come there to do? "Yeah. I'm sorry about that." Lying there in the semi-darkness, he couldn't help that he felt there was a divide they would never cross, that she didn't want to stay with him, even if he might be the last person on Earth.

"For what?" she asked, oblivious to his distress.

How could he tell her? "That I'm not…someone you feel comfortable staying with, I guess."

"What?" she asked again, obviously confused. She turned again, this time to face him.

"You said you wanted us to go on with our lives. I thought you meant to go our separate ways." He hoped his tone wasn't overly bitter.

She surprised him by softening her expression. "No. I don't want you to think that. I don't want you to go. I just meant that we could find somewhere comfortable to stay and grow our own food. I don't want to rely on cans of…stuff… forever."

Relieved, he let out his breath. "Me, neither."

"Maybe we could find a house somewhere. Not here. I don't want to see Smithton Lake ever again." She wiped her hair out of her eyes and had a thoughtful expression.

"Sounds great. Maybe we can get a place on the beach. How about that? It would've cost a fortune before, but I'll bet we can get one now. Not that this is the way I'd want it to happen, of course."

"We still need a garden. I want to grow vegetables," she insisted.

"Well, sure. That would be amazing." He thought a while. Did he have anything on his wish list? "I want an art studio," he mused.

"Why?"

"What do you mean? I like to paint. I'm not just a photographer." He felt slightly indignant but tried not to show it.

"No. I mean, because no one will be able to buy your paintings, so why do you want to make them?"

Shaking his head, he didn't know how to explain it to her. "I don't do it only for the money. I do it because I enjoy it and just because I want to. It's almost like a compulsion. I couldn't stop if I wanted to."

"Okay. We'll have an art studio." she agreed.

"Thank you," he responded, although he wasn't sure what he was thanking her for. For indulging him? For understanding? Either way, he was grateful that they were making plans for the future. Hopefully, it wasn't a pointless exercise.

———

When darkness fell completely around the lake, they could hear the familiar and yet terrifying sounds of the skeletons patrolling the area. Jackson could hear them approaching the house, suddenly feeling a twinge like intuition that something was different this time. Something was wrong. He quietly urged Nadine out of bed and into the closet, hearing noises at the windows and doors like the skeletons were attempting to gain entry. The barricades held, but Jackson knew they might not last the night.

He pointed upward, although Nadine couldn't possibly see the gesture in the blackness, he hoped she'd surely sensed his movement. Reaching up toward the ceiling, he felt a string attached to a light, then a smooth wooden panel to the left of it. Thankful for the somewhat low ceiling in the closet, he slid the panel to the side and lifted Nadine to climb through the opening into the attic crawlspace above them. Once he was sure she was safe, he reached up and struggled to climb upward, hearing a crash in the living room as one of the barriers toppled over. Hundreds of the skeletons were marching around the house. He could hear them. But he forced himself to be silent as he climbed up and then slid the panel back into place behind him, holding onto Nadine. His hands shook as he could hear scurrying and scratching in the pitch blackness, some unknown critters or insects being upset that someone else was in their territory. But Jackson couldn't think about it. He knew their lives were in danger from the skeletons and not any pests.

Metallic footsteps sounded inside the house as the skeletons searched as if they were aware someone was there. Perhaps the barricades were a clue, but Jackson hoped they would believe the inhabitants had fled. Then, the closet door below them opened, and he tried his best to quiet his breathing. Nadine would have cried out if his hand hadn't been over her mouth. Jackson didn't say a word and only held her, holding his breath as he listened intently, trying not to make a sound.

Then, the footsteps moved away, almost hesitantly, as if they still sensed someone was present. But they wandered the house below, several of them, and Jackson wished he had been able to bring a weapon up with him. However, it lay uselessly beside the bed where he and Nadine had been trying to sleep. He forced himself to breathe slowly and deeply, wishing the night were over so that the things would go back to wherever they went during the day.

Hours passed, but the skeletons were still there.

Sometimes they passed the closet or even stepped inside. Don't look up, Jackson prayed. Don't look up. He could feel tiny insect legs crawling on his arms, but he didn't dare react or move, couldn't move. Anything he did could give himself or Nadine away, and their lives would end. He couldn't let anything happen to Nadine, not now that he'd supposedly saved her once. But was he just prolonging the inevitable? Would she die when they breached the structure over the lake? Would he? Would he end up leaving her to brave the terrible new world alone? He tried not to think of it, instead focusing on his breaths, keeping them slow and even and trying to keep Nadine calm.

He wanted to slide backward into the safety of the blackness behind him, but he feared that any movement he made would sound below like a klaxon giving away his presence. Shivering slightly, he willed the metallic things to go away, willed them to believe the house was empty. Part of him knew it was ridiculous, but he wanted to believe he had some control over the situation. Go away, he thought. Go away.

And when morning finally came, they went away, slowly at first, only lessening their numbers outside. The few skeletons that had entered the house were reluctant, as if they still sensed their quarry was nearby. However, they, too, eventually left the house, perhaps knowing they still had another opportunity to find the humans as if they were saying, "We'll find you yet."

————

CHAPTER

TEN

"Why do we still need to go to the dome?" Nadine wanted to know. She sat, eating a pastry, at the dining table with the blinds drawn closed. The door with the view of the lake was blocked off days before, also. They had rebuilt the breached barricade once morning had come.

"I want to know if there's a simple way to disable those skeletons or to destroy them. As you pointed out, the EMP won't destroy all of them, only the ones in close proximity to it. So, we need to first find out if there is a simpler solution." Jackson handed her a bottle of water and sat down across from her. She'd already opened his pastry and left it by his usual chair, even though his arm was healing by then, but he was strangely grateful for the gesture and hoped it meant things were improving between the two of them.

"Couldn't we set off the bomb first and then go in?" she worried.

"No, because if there is anything with any electrical circuits or technology in it, it won't function anymore once we've set off the bomb. If we want to use it to disable *all* of the skeletons, we need it to be in working order." He took a bite of his pastry and began to fully understand her desire for fresh food. Being used to processed food was one thing, but enjoying it was an entirely different experience.

She frowned, but she looked like she was still thinking. "Then we still need a boat. We didn't get a boat," she pointed out.

"Yeah," he said unhappily. "I'm aware of that."

"Do we need to go back to the base?" she asked.

Trying to decide if she was being facetious, he looked into her eyes and realized she was just planning their day. "Yeah, I suppose we should. And we need to go as early as we can. I don't want anyone to find out we're here."

"No. I don't either," she agreed, crinkling her empty wrapper and standing to put it into the trash.

He looked down and saw that he'd only taken one bite of his breakfast, so he reluctantly finished it in a couple of large gulps, then he took his water with him as they hurried out to the passenger car that they'd taken from the auto repair garage a few days earlier. Fishing the keys out of his pocket, he unlocked the doors and quickly sat down, starting the engine as soon as Nadine was beside him with her seatbelt secured. Jackson felt exposed out in the driveway, but he carefully reversed onto the road and then sped away toward the long dirt path leading to the military base.

———

The gate was still open as they approached, and they drove straight in and toward the water, where they'd seen the boats docked the day before. Jackson didn't want to leave the car behind, but he also knew that once they'd set off the bomb, it wouldn't work anymore anyway. His earlier argument with Nadine seemed all the more pointless, and he wished he hadn't snapped at her. He didn't know if the Humvee would work either, so they would probably be stuck on foot until they could get far enough away from the site to find an operational vehicle, which didn't sound appealing at all. Would they stand a chance anyway? He didn't want to think they didn't.

The boat still floated in the water near the shore, so Jackson helped Nadine into it, then he handed her their bags of weapons before climbing aboard and preparing to leave. He untied the rope, then they both examined the controls to determine how to operate them. It was far more complicated than any boat Jackson had ever been on, but it wasn't an ocean-faring vessel, so he assumed it could have been far more complex. He turned the key, sat down at the helm, then turned the wheel to pull away from the dock.

The massive dome was visible from the entire area, and it loomed in the distance as they approached. The whining noise they'd noticed when they'd first arrived was still prevalent, and it worried them immensely. Jackson tried to see if there were any signs they'd been spotted or were being expected, but he couldn't tell from so far away. He still didn't know how to gain entry either, and he worried that the weapons they had weren't enough.

The closer they got to the structure, the louder the whine seemed to get. Jackson couldn't determine if it were because they were closer to the source or if it were a warning of some sort. He was afraid the skeletons could still get to them, even halfway across the lake. Also, he worried there would be more skeletons in the structure when they managed to get inside. Mostly, he feared what would happen if they failed.

When they were almost to the stilts, the only part they could reach, they could see that the entire structure was covered in a thin layer of mud, as if it had once hidden beneath the lake. Were there other structures like this elsewhere? How long had they been there? What was their purpose? Jackson hoped they would find out, but he also thought their first priority was to disable the skeletons or, better yet, destroy them.

They brought the boat alongside one of the legs and looked for some sort of entry point or anything that might serve as one. The structure was unfathomably large, and it loomed above them. Jackson looked up from the boat and up at the light-colored underside of the dome. The coloration almost reminded him of a shark, with the upper dome a slightly darker shade. The legs seemed more angular than the somewhat dome-shaped upper part of the structure, and they were light-colored like the underside of the rest of the frame.

However, to his dismay, the entire thing was seamless, and he couldn't discern anything they might use to get inside. It was urgent now. They had given away their existence, and the skeletons could probably track them back to their hiding place and the vehicle, their only transportation. He had no idea how to gain a replacement.

They made their way to another leg and then another. Nothing looked any different. It was all angular but smooth. The skeletons must have another way to get inside, he assumed. Wishing he had explosives, he looked to see what sort of weapons the military boat possessed. There were guns, but not torpedoes or anything of that sort. Deciding that they had no choice but to attempt entry by force, Jackson fired the boat's guns at the strange structure in front of them, hearing several loud bangs as each shot rang against the metal. He closed his eyes to protect them from any shrapnel or debris, worrying that he had made their arrival abundantly obvious. What if the skeletons were now massing inside the dome, waiting to meet them? Pausing a moment, he stopped firing and peered over the front of the boat to see what had actually occurred. There was a jagged hole in the leg of the dome, revealing only a black space beyond. Jackson looked back to Nadine, who appeared terrified, but she gave him a nod anyway. He brought the boat alongside the damaged leg, then leaned across until he could almost see inside. It seemed lit from within, and he could see steps leading upward. Pulling back, he dropped the anchor for the boat alongside the leg to keep it from drifting away. Taking a bag of weapons, he also took Nadine's hand and helped her onto the lower step right behind him. They took several deep breaths to steady themselves, feeling terror as they entered the alien structure. When Jackson turned, however, he could still see the boat tied outside, waiting for their return. Well, that was a relief, actually.

Nadine took one of the machine guns as quietly as she could, and then they both climbed the stairs, listening as the whine grew louder and louder until it felt like their ears were full of water. But they kept going, up the strange steps that glowed as the walls lit up. Jackson reached into the bag and withdrew a weapon as they neared the top. It felt like hours later. But the two of them, then, carefully peered into a long, curved hallway. Eventually, they saw that it led to a large room that appeared empty as they entered it. They walked cautiously around the space, afraid there would be skeletons, or worse, inside. But they saw no one. Jackson tried listening for footsteps, but the whine was so intense that he could hear nothing else.

He quickly scanned the large grey room, but around him were only flat steel walls with no adornment and nothing that looked like a computer terminal or access hatch or anything of the sort. The cyborgs (because that must be what they were, as they had organic and synthetic parts) must have some sort of controls somewhere for them to be able to operate. Since the cyborgs had always known where he and Nadine were going as if they could somehow communicate with each other, it made sense to him. What if that was done from here?

Nadine was getting antsy. He could see it in her eyes and in her gestures. She was ready to leave. But he hadn't figured it out. He hadn't accomplished anything. He kept going around the room, trying to find what they'd come for. Was it even possible to do anything from there?

Frustrated, he walked toward the center of the space, walking around a corner and then a wall of light rose up between himself and Nadine. He spun around, pounding his hands on the wall, but his hands felt like they had struck metal as they didn't pass through. He started to panic, feeling trapped and also scared that something would happen to Nadine and he couldn't protect her. Trying to call out to her, he couldn't hear his own voice, almost like a dream he'd had when he was a child. That meant he couldn't hear her either, so he had no idea if she were alive or dead. Was she alone on the other side of the wall? He hoped she was safe, but he couldn't be sure. He wanted to be sure.

Then, he turned to the solid metal wall behind him, wondering if there was a way to go around it and back to where Nadine might be in danger. However, part of him was terrified that he would run into something far worse if he left his place. Walking around the space, he tried to see if there were controls or anything that might bring the light wall down. He hit the metal wall panels with his palms and swiped around near what almost looked like another room with a chair-like structure in the center. Still nothing. He looked behind him, and the wall of light was still there. He hunted for an exit, but he couldn't see that there was any opening in the light wall, despite his frantic searching and pounding on it. It rose as high as the ceiling in the space, and he knew he couldn't just go over it. He felt desperation take over and slid to the floor, nearly breaking down. He had no idea how to get out, and he had no idea if he could stop the skeletons from finding out where he was.

Suddenly, he heard the unmistakable sound of metallic footsteps on the other side of the wall, even over the loud whining that made his ears hurt. "No!" he screamed, fearing for Nadine. Then, fearing that he may have given away his location, despite not being able to hear a word from his own mouth, he tried to control his breathing. What if the skeletons could hear better than he could? Surely the loud whine had a purpose. He didn't think the skeletons would be able to do what they could do if they couldn't operate in spite of it.

Then, there was an opening in the wall of light, and he quickly crawled behind the chair in the new room that he had been experimenting with moments earlier. He heard footsteps come closer, but they paused. Then, he could hear them moving around the space, and he tried to disappear, to keep on the other side of the chair and out of sight. He hoped to work his way close to the exit, but he wasn't sure, even then, that he wouldn't be spotted if he ran. Even worse, he wasn't sure how many skeletons were out there and if he wouldn't just be killed on the other side of the light wall if he escaped. Eventually, he heard the steps cross to the opening again, and then the opening was gone. He felt his heart break at the thought that he was trapped there forever and also that he would never know what had happened to Nadine.

He stood and began pounding on the metal wall behind him again, still trying to hide behind the chair, but nothing happened. What was it for? He felt like it must be important. The chair faced it for some reason. It wouldn't just face a blank wall, would it? He looked around on the sides, and his fingers touched what felt like a small indention in the smooth surface. Suddenly, the color of the light changed from a greenish grey to a bright white-yellow, and an alarm sounded, then the opening in the light wall was back. He dropped back to the floor, hearing the metallic footsteps again enter the space on the other side.

Had he found something? Or had he triggered the alarm himself? He looked up at the wall in front of the chair and could see glowing symbols, like futuristic pictographs, etched into the surface. They almost reminded him of Mayan glyphs, but not quite. He had no idea what they meant, but he didn't recall seeing them there before. He closed his eyes briefly, fearing what would happen if he miscalculated, then he touched one of the symbols, feeling as if he were out of options.

As one, the skeletons converged on the chair, a screeching sound emanating from what had been their mouths when they had looked human. There was only a gaping hole in the metallic heads, and the lights in their eyes brightened. He knew he was dead. He knew it was too late, and he would be ripped apart like Nadine's boyfriend, David.

Then, gunfire resounded and echoed throughout the room. He remembered the gun in his hands but was too afraid to shoot the metallic creatures at close range. Looking up at them, he was overjoyed to see Nadine's angry visage appear behind the cyborgs, firing her weapon into their heads above him. He ducked lower and covered his head and neck, trying to protect himself as bits of the skeletons showered over him. Then, Nadine took a hand to shove the remaining parts aside, taking Jackson's arm and helping him stand. He could now

see that there were symbols in the air and covering the wall,
as well. He wanted to kill them. He wanted to kill all of them.
How could he do so without destroying himself and Nadine
in the process? He had no idea if he could shut them all down
permanently. But he wasn't sure that was good enough. He
feared they could just "reboot" and then begin their assault
on humanity once again.

Shaking his head, he knew he had to do something,
but he also knew it could be a mistake. Sighing, he touched a
symbol as it floated in front of him in the air, thinking he had
to try something after they'd come so far and been through so
much, even if it backfired. And then, the wall of light dropped
into the floor, and he could see the skeletons on the other
side. They all turned to face him, and then advanced across
the room. He shook his head and touched another symbol
and then another. It didn't seem to make a difference. The
skeletons screeched as they approached him, their glowing
eyes malevolent.

He lifted his weapon and fired into the skeletons'
heads, feeling Nadine turn her back to his and fire in the other
direction. He knew they couldn't escape. There were too
many skeletons and only two humans with a few guns. The
skeletons in the front ranks had fallen, but the ones behind
would only brush their mechanical corpses aside and keep
coming. Nadine covered him as he tried swiping the air and
touching symbols embedded in the wall, but when his fingers
touched them, the symbols didn't appear as before. Instead,
they seemed to dim. He didn't know if that was a good thing
or not, but he felt like he may have found some sort of control
center. He wished he knew how to work it, but he couldn't
stop firing long enough to explore its possibilities further.

Nadine reloaded with Jackson covering her, but then suddenly, she smacked the wall with the palm of her hand in anger, and the skeletons began to luminesce. Jackson could feel the heat coming off them, and he hoped they would destruct. However, although they moved in a more stilted manner, they were still moving. He paused briefly to fire madly into the crowd of skeletons, screaming at the unfairness of it all. Nothing happened.

Nadine was firing again, and she looked like she had been crying, but he knew she was angry with him. He had failed her. She had wanted to hide forever, and he had made her come here. It was all his fault. Her death was on him.

"What do you *want*?" he shouted ineffectually at the mass of metal beings in front of him.

"Your planet," came an answer from nowhere. It echoed as if it had always existed, and he just had never heard it before. The skeletons seemed to pause their attack as the voice sounded in the room, the whine becoming less prominent.

"It isn't yours! It belongs to us!" he shouted back to the faceless voice.

"It doesn't appear to belong to you," said the Voice.

"We were here first!" Jackson countered.

"That never stopped you. Your people conquered other people when the land was already taken," the Voice replied.

"Where did you come from? Who are you?" Jackson asked, unsure it really mattered anymore. But he would have some answers, at last, he thought.

"We are from the Emptiness. We need a planet of our own."

He wasn't sure that meant anything to anyone but the

skeletons. "Why did you look human before?"

"We had to pass as citizens to avoid destruction. You are easy to imitate."

He didn't know why, but he felt supremely insulted for all humans. "Then why did you start to rot? Why can we see you for what you are now?"

"The lab created a plague to detect us. We destroyed them."

"Why are you still here? You've killed everyone! Isn't that what you wanted?" Jackson shouted, indignant.

"We need your planet. Your people are irrelevant."

"What is the Emptiness? Why do you need our planet?" Jackson asked finally, trying to clarify.

"The Emptiness is our home. It is a place devoid of worlds. We need a world so that we may live."

"That doesn't answer my question! Why do you need our world?"

"We need any world. Your world was easy to conquer. We will live here forever and multiply."

Jackson felt lost. It still didn't make sense. "You could have taken an uninhabited world. Why Earth?"

"It has the requirements we need to survive."

Then, something occurred to him. "Can you share? Why can't you share this world with us? How many of you are here?"

"There are many of us. We need the entire world."

"So, you're not just in Smithton Lake? You're everywhere?"

"Yes," came the Voice.

"Why did you chase us? Why did you care about the two of us?" Jackson asked then, enjoying the brief pause

while the Voice deigned to speak to him, and the attacks had
subsided.

"We no longer needed you."

"But before, you did?" Jackson was confused.

"We feared attack and destruction. We pretended and
hid in plain sight. Once we were exposed, we no longer felt
the need to hide."

Nadine stood behind him, shivering slightly and
shifting position, but she waited. Jackson didn't look back.
He was trying to stall the skeletons while he thought of an
escape plan.

"But why the two of us?" he still tried to clarify. "Why
do you need to kill us? We aren't a threat to you! We're
nothing!"

"But you are here. That proves you are a threat. No
human is insignificant. You must all be eradicated."

Something clicked in Jackson at that reply. No. They
were not insignificant. They wouldn't be. "What is this place?"
Jackson asked, not expecting a real answer.

"Us," the Voice said.

"How?" But he thought he knew. "A control center?"
There was no further reply, and he knew he'd found the
solution.

But Nadine suddenly held the last few of the stun
guns to the wall behind her in front of the chair and activated
them simultaneously, watching as the luminescing skeletons
suddenly began screeching anew, the panel bathed in blue
light as the guns' energy destroyed the beacon in the wall's
controls and preventing the skeletons from receiving new
instructions. The screeching intensified, and the skeletons
vibrated violently, pointing at Jackson accusingly as they

began to freeze and grow silent where they stood. Nadine screamed, and he took her arm to calm her. The screeching slowly died away as the skeletons' forms seemed to lock up and become still. However, the light and heat remained. There were piles of glowing, hot metal all around them as some of the skeletons toppled over, and they felt sweat drip down their faces as they looked upon the destruction they had wrought. But was it enough?

Jackson looked back at the wall and saw that the controls, again, had changed and were now red. The strange glyphs showed up in the corner of it, switching rapidly, but he could see that the number of symbols was slowly decreasing.

"Erm--I think this is a countdown!" he yelled to Nadine. A countdown to what was the big question. But Jackson took Nadine's arm and guided her back around to the curved hallway at a run toward their original entrance point. It was getting harder to concentrate. A new sound came through the whine, and the lighting seemed to change to red, imitating the strange glyphs they had seen in the control center. They turned to go down the stairs, racing through the space as the heat grew.

Jackson backed carefully down, checking behind him as he went to be sure Nadine was safe. When they neared the bottom, he was afraid the hole they had made would have been blocked off, but it was still gaping in front of them. They both tumbled into the boat in their haste, and Jackson quickly pulled up the anchor. He pushed the boat away, started the engine, and aimed the boat toward the shore. They raced as quickly as they could across the water. He wasn't sure how much time they had or if they needed to worry at all. He just wanted to get away. Nadine was crying and shivering, but he had no way to comfort her. He just kept the engine going and headed for the house on the hill.

By the time they were a little closer to the shore, he had started to wonder if it had been worth it after all. Nothing happened. Nothing had changed. They would probably still have to run. But the alarm still sounded. Then suddenly, the dome collapsed in on itself. He heard it before he saw it. Turning to look upon hearing the sonic boom, like an implosion, he watched as the thing just crumpled into the lake, looking almost like tin foil but releasing smoke and flames as it went down. Jackson felt a small amount of satisfaction knowing that the skeletons that had been inside were crushed along with the structure, and he feared what would be going on back on land. Then, the aftershock hit them, and waves threatened to overtake the boat as it began rocking heavily in the waves.

In the end, he didn't quite reach the pier behind the house but ran the boat up into the mud as they sprinted for the back door, intending to reach the Humvee, but they saw that the ground was littered with glowing skeletons. The skeletons seemed to have just fallen wherever they'd been and were smoldering in the grass. Small fires were starting all over the hillside, and acrid smoke rose in the air, stinging their eyes and lungs as they ran. There had been hundreds of them waiting. Jackson and Nadine held the last of their weapons at the ready as they ran toward the rear door, reached it, and ran through the door into the garage, where Jackson quickly unlocked the sliding door and slid it upward. Then, Nadine practically leaped into the Humvee. Jackson carefully stowed his weapon before going to the EMP and looking for a switch or a timer, setting it for thirty minutes to give them time to get away. Hurriedly, he started the Humvee and sped away. He never wanted to see Smithton Lake ever again. He never intended to go back after that day. However, he felt drawn back to the lab. He wanted to recover his lost camera, although he didn't know why, but he also felt he needed to have some sort of ammunition against the skeletons should the skeletons ever return.

They knew the bomb had detonated as they drove further from the lake, watching the time on the clock on the dashboard. Jackson was immensely grateful that the Humvee's electrical equipment was shielded, at least to some degree. When his watch went dead, the second hand freezing as if time itself had stopped, he knew it was done, and he hoped they would be safe for the first time in several days. Relieved, he drove around the lake until they reached the area that he'd fled so many days ago. As the vehicle approached the lab complex, Jackson could see the remnants of other cars and trucks in the lot, the debris from previous altercations with the cyborgs. He was surprised to find that the case with his camera was still abandoned on the concrete. Knowing the SLR was probably no longer operable, he retrieved it for the view camera alone, then continued in the Humvee up onto the concourse and up to the building where the lab was located.

He took one of the last of the guns with him, with only one extra magazine left, as he searched through the building, climbing the stairs to the third floor rather than using the disabled elevator. Entering the lab wasn't difficult. Although he didn't want to draw attention to himself, just in case, he fired a bullet into the lock and made his way into the outer office. Nadine followed him timidly inside, checking over her shoulder as she covered their rear with her last gun. Reaching the inner office, Jackson again fired into the lock and entered the dark space, unable to use the now-dead flashlights as the EMP had destroyed their electronic components. He fumbled around in the blackness, where only dim light showed through the metal blinds over the windows until he could find the cabinets where the artifacts had been stored and broke the lock. He wasn't sure what he would do with the objects when he found them, but he found he was afraid to touch them upon seeing them again. He just stood there.

Nadine was searching through a desk, and he heard the rustling of papers. He turned to try to peer over her shoulder and began to read documents, standing in the faint light from the window as he drew up the blinds. She handed him a stack of papers, and, at first, he didn't understand what he was reading, but he soon realized that the memos and reports he read referred to a virus that the lab had developed. The reports referenced the numbers assigned to the artifacts in the cabinets that he had previously photographed. Did that mean the artifacts were used to develop the virus? He wasn't sure. But the more he read, the more that seemed to be the case. Had the lab suspected something before the night he saw the strange people in the shuttle? He found a briefcase and began stuffing any documents that seemed relevant into it, then took some of the artifacts carefully out of the cabinets using blank paper to wrap them, and put them into the briefcase, as well. He wanted to be prepared should they ever need the technology again.

They made their way cautiously back down to the Humvee, and Jackson loaded the briefcase and their remaining weapons into the back seat before driving away.

But as they drove, they could see that the skeletons

seemed to be dead. They didn't know for how long. They didn't know if there were other facilities like the one in Smithton Lake. He could only guess. But he and Nadine raced away from the city, swerving the car around the metal skeletons they encountered lying on the roads.

He didn't know where to go. But he aimed the car toward the east and kept driving on toward the horizon, the sun setting on their past behind them. But the stars glittered ahead of them like the jewels of new opportunities.

As they drove toward the coast, Jackson and Nadine met others who had somehow managed to hide long enough that the skeletons had not found them. As they slowly emerged from their hiding places once the skeletons were frozen, Jackson told them about his adventures with Nadine, how they had found an EMP device and disabled the skeletons near Smithton Lake. He and Nadine still warily carried weapons everywhere with them, not sure what to expect from the others or if there were still skeletons somewhere nearby. However, as word very slowly spread about how to disable the skeletons for good (as many people feared the skeletons would just reboot even after the beacon was destroyed), they either found e-bombs or built some themselves and used them against the invaders (if they didn't simply dismantle them once they'd cooled), finding they wanted a more permanent solution than the destroyed beacon would provide. The skeletons numbers dwindled as the frozen machines were disassembled and torn apart. It seemed fitting to Nadine, who still bore mental scars from her ordeal the night they'd first attacked.

However, only five years later, the attack began to fade from people's foremost thoughts. Many of the survivors were wary of others and traumatized. And although the people had initially been skeptical of one another, they knew, in the end, that they needed each other. Small communities began to form, where they were organizing themselves into primitive tribes. Most of them were initially somewhat nomadic, but some knew how to grow food, and those settled into the remnants of the small towns, fortified with makeshift walls with the gardens and farms toward the outskirts.

Jackson and Nadine never returned to the Smithton Lake area. They continued driving, staying in abandoned hotels or anything else they could make comfortable until they reached the east coast. Carefully, they searched the towns until they found a small cottage on the beach that was in reasonably good condition. It was a two-bedroom house on stilts with wood siding that had weathered slightly. So, they set about repairing any damage, and Jackson helped Nadine put plant pots and a garden plot behind the house so they could grow their own food. With help from the local library, which he finally located and explored, he also built a brick oven in the yard so that they could cook the food they'd grown.

Eventually, once their basic needs were being met, Jackson built a shed in the back and stocked it with found art supplies from a nearby craft store. It wasn't a priority, but he enjoyed getting back to doing something simply because he wanted to. His paintings were abstract landscapes, colorful and melancholy at the same time, inspired by their journey to the sea. Nadine indulged him, and his paintings graced the walls of their quaint little cottage once they were completed.

One of the things they hadn't thought of previously was how they could watch the sunrise over the ocean from their front porch. It was a luxury they had never imagined they needed, but then they couldn't imagine doing without.

But the main thing that Jackson struggled with was gratitude. How could he ever thank Nadine for saving him? He'd saved her once, and she'd saved him many times over in return. He only knew he would probably spend the rest of his life trying to express his feelings simply because words were not enough.

Jackson and Nadine weren't sure if they would end up as a couple, but they didn't want to be separated, so perhaps that was a sign. However, they were both grieving and had suffered unimaginable losses, and they knew they both needed time. But as they watched their garden grow, they were optimistic for the first time since they had defeated the cyborgs.

One morning, Nadine saw small white and yellow daisies growing outside their door Carefully, she used a spade to remove a few of them with the roots intact, along with some of the soil. Then, she planted them in an old glass jar and set them in the new kitchen window, smiling as the colorful blossoms made her feel like she'd brought rays of sunshine into the house.

———————

ACKNOWLEDGEMENTS

Many people helped to make this book a reality, and I would like to thank everyone who contributed, in one way or another, throughout the entire process. I really appreciate everyone who picked up a copy, whether from your local bookseller, an online retailer, or even your local library. You are the reason I do what I do. Thank you. I only hope you enjoy reading the book as much as I enjoyed writing it.

But naturally, I have a few people I would like to name specifically. First, I would like to thank Hermione Lee for her insight and enthusiasm. I might have given up on this story if it hadn't been for her help. Her suggestions were invaluable. Also, Heather Dixon provided much-appreciated support when I most needed it, and I can't thank her enough. Inge Pratt encouraged me to pursue this endeavor at the start, so I have her to thank for even beginning the journey to publication. My father, Alfredo Peña, as always, is my biggest fan. Thank you, Daddy. I love you. My sister Michelle Kollin, brother-in-law Mike Kollin, and my mother Charlotte Peña kept my morale up, even when things became very difficult. I appreciate that more than you know. Obviously, I can't wait for next Halloween!

In this novel, I know I couldn't have provided the detail needed for the opening sequence without Neil Maurer's view camera class in college. It was one of my favorite classes (as were many of Mr. Maurer's), but as always, any errors are my own. And, of course, this novel wouldn't be what it is without Karen Fuller and her fabulous editing. I am not infallible, and

I appreciate her help in making this book the best it can be. Last, but certainly not least, I would like to thank everyone at World Castle Publishing. You are amazing!

ABOUT THE AUTHOR

Cheryl Peña was born in San Antonio, Texas, to a Hispanic-American father and a British-American mother. She developed an early interest in art and language, winning first place in the National Language Arts Olympiad when she was 11 years old. She studied art and photography at the University of Texas–San Antonio, graduating with honors in 2000. Upon the death of her twin sister in 2014, she decided to write professionally in her sister's honor. Her first novella, a suspense thriller titled *The House of Wynne Lift,* was published in 2021 and won the Literary Titan Gold Book Award. *Descent of the Vile* is her first novel.

www.ingramcontent.com/pod-product-compliance
Lightning Source LLC
Chambersburg PA
CBHW030335180626
46810CB00003B/1373